DOWN B[barcode]

Fargo lay with his head filled with flashes of colored light. But he wasn't unconscious. He could see the three men who had turned their attention to Caroline, holding her down.

Fargo spotted a pitchfork nearby. He pulled it toward him. Then he reached into the calf holster around his leg and drew the thin, double-edged throwing knife called an Arkansas toothpick.

A pitchfork and a knife. Not much to take care of three armed and vicious killers. But right now they'd have to do the job—the job the Trailsman aimed to do even if he had just his naked hands. . . .

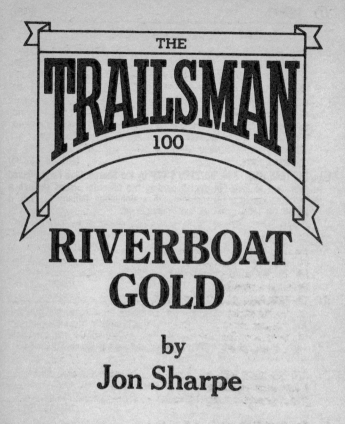

THE
TRAILSMAN
100

RIVERBOAT
GOLD

by
Jon Sharpe

A SIGNET BOOK

SIGNET
Published by the Penguin Group
Penguin Books USA Inc., 375 Hudson Street,
New York, New York 10014, U.S.A.
Penguin Books Ltd, 27 Wrights Lane,
London W8 5TZ, England
Penguin Books Australia Ltd, Ringwood,
Victoria, Australia
Penguin Books Canada Ltd, 2801 John Street,
Markham, Ontario, Canada L3R 1B4
Penguin Books (N.A.) Ltd, 182–190 Wairau Road,
Auckland 10, New Zealand

Penguin Books Ltd, Registered Offices:
Harmondsworth, Middlesex, England

First published by Signet, an imprint of Penguin Books USA Inc.

First Printing, April, 1990
10 9 8 7 6 5 4 3 2 1

The first chapter of this book previously appeared in Camp St. Lucifer, the ninety-ninth volume in this series.

REGISTERED TRADEMARK—MARCA REGISTRADA

Printed in the United States of America

PUBLISHER'S NOTE
This is a work of fiction. Names, characters, places, and incidents either are the product of the author's imagination or are used fictitiously, and any resemblance to actual persons, living or dead, events, or locales is entirely coincidental.

BOOKS ARE AVAILABLE AT QUANTITY DISCOUNTS WHEN USED TO PROMOTE PRODUCTS OR SERVICES. FOR INFORMATION PLEASE WRITE TO PREMIUM MARKETING DIVISION, PENGUIN BOOKS USA INC., 375 HUDSON STREET, NEW YORK, NEW YORK 10014

The Trailsman

Beginnings . . . they bend the tree and they mark the man. Skye Fargo was born when he was eighteen. Terror was his midwife, vengeance his first cry. Killing spawned Skye Fargo, ruthless, cold-blooded murder. Out of the acrid smoke of gunpowder still hanging in the air, he rose, cried out a promise never forgotten.

The Trailsman, they began to call him, all across the West: searcher, scout, hunter, the man who could see where others only looked, his skills for hire but not his soul, the man who lived each day to the fullest, yet trailed each tomorrow. Skye Fargo, the Trailsman, the seeker who could take the wildness of a land and the wanting of a woman and make them his own.

*1860, a time when the future
had already wrapped the land in its long,
grim shadow and killing was as much
an omen as an act . . .*

1

"No, you hear me? No!"

"We just thought it might be easier if we dry-gulched him before he reached the cabin, like halfway down the hill."

"You stay out of sight on top of the hill and that's all you do. This is no ordinary cowpoke. This is Skye Fargo, the Trailsman. This is a man who can outtrail the Pawnee, outfox the Comanche, and outfight the Crow. Some say he's part cougar and part hawk. You four try ambushing him anywhere near that cabin and he'll see you, hear you, smell you, or just plain feel you. While you're waiting, he'll have you in his sights."

"It was a thought."

"A goddamn dumb one. You stay on top of the hill and wait. I've five men who're going to try to take him along the way. If they don't do it, then we wait till he's in the cabin with the girl. That'll be your only chance to take him, when his attention is on the girl. After you take him, you bring him to me. We know he got the letter, but we don't know how much was in it. You got it all straight now?"

"Yes, sir."

"You stay hidden on top of the hill, watch the cabin for the signal, and then move in. That'll be your only chance to take him. You stick to the goddamn plan. It's been carefully worked out. Now get moving."

The man's eyebrows, thick, bushy, and black, knitted together as he watched the others hurry away. He spat in disgust.

The big man rode casually, not hurrying, sitting easily astride the magnificent Ovaro, the horse's jet-black fore- and hindquarters glistening in the sun, his pure-white midsection agleam. Lake-blue eyes scanned the terrain with deceptive casualness as Skye Fargo rode and the echo of a smile edged his lips. They'd been following him all day, he was aware, through the north Iowa country southward. It was good riding country: gentle hills, mostly flatland, sparsely timbered with shadbush and slippery elm. Five riders, he'd counted. They had kept apart and stayed back, as if that was all there was to trailing someone.

Amateurs, Fargo grunted. They didn't know how to follow the far side of a rock formation or move through the thick tree stands without showing their path. And they didn't know enough not to keep the same pace. They'd been easy to spot, not that they realized it. But they were cautious enough not to move closer in the open country and so he had continued on with seeming unawareness. The day passed into the afternoon and he watched the terrain change character, grow thicker with good stands of box elder, shagbark hickory, and black walnut. He guessed that the Mississippi flowed some ten miles to his left and he turned the pinto westward toward a long stretch of thick forest, mostly shagbark hickory. He liked hickory forests with their supply of appetizing nuts ready for the taking, the sweet insides worth fighting through the thick husks.

He sent the Ovaro into the denseness of the forest, scanned the good, thick underbrush, and glanced back to see the five riders start to hurry forward, instantly fearful of losing their quarry. They were dependent on sight, another mark of the amateur.

Fargo spotted a break in the trees and rode into it. He paused, gave them a chance to see him before he turned back into the woods. The five riders had moved in close to one another now, certain the thick forest was the place they had waited for, their chance to strike. Fargo paused, listened, heard them closing fast, already into the forest. They were amateur trackers but probably far from amateur gunslingers, he realized. His chiseled countenance tightened. It was time to give them a chance to do what they'd come to do.

He half-turned the pinto and sent the horse through the dense underbrush at a fast canter and heard his pursuers change direction at once to take after him. As the Ovaro crashed through the thick brush, Fargo pulled his left leg over the saddle and half-jumped, half-slid from the horse, his lariat in one hand. He landed on the balls of his feet and immediately sank down into the thick brush as the Ovaro raced on. Two of his pursuers came into sight almost at once, riding hard, skirting thick-trunked hickories, a third close on their heels. Fargo waited, had the lariat half-raised in one hand as the last two appeared. He let the first one go by, then half-rose and flung the lariat as the last horseman passed by. The Trailsman caught the glance of astonishment in the man's face as the noose landed around his shoulders, tightened, and yanked him from the saddle.

"Goddamn," the man cursed as he hit the ground, but Fargo was at him in three long strides. He crashed the butt of the Colt onto the man's head, and the figure went limp. He'd stay that way until it was time to question him. Fargo saw the other horseman coming back toward him, alerted by his partner's curse. Fargo raised the Colt, fired, and the rider half-rose in the saddle before he pitched backward from his horse, a red hole in the middle of his chest.

The shot would bring the other three, Fargo knew, and he stepped back from the figure wrapped in the lariat, his eyes narrowed as he peered through the trees. The other three horsemen took only another half-minute to reappear, charging back toward him. He dropped to one knee, raised the Colt, and fired again. The one in the center toppled from his horse as though yanked by an invisible wire, but the other two dived headlong from their saddles to land heavily in the brush. Fargo heard them roll, and he dropped onto his stomach as a spray of bullets flew in his general direction.

He pushed backward on his stomach, found the gray-barked thick trunk of an old hickory, and pushed himself behind it. The two men had stopped shooting, no doubt to reload.

Staying behind the wide, thick trunk, Fargo raised his voice. "Talk and you can walk," he called out. "Who sent you after me?" The answer, not unexpected, sent woodchips flying from the tree as another volley of shots exploded. Fargo grimaced, yet stayed put. The gunfire ended and he called out again. "You're being stupid," he said. This time a single shot answered him, the bullet hitting the other side of the thick tree trunk with a dull thud.

12

Fargo remained in place and he had but a few minutes to wait before he heard their whispered exchange. Another minute passed until he heard the two men begin to push their way forward through the thick underbrush. His eyes narrowed as he let his ears see for him; he stayed motionless behind the thick trunk. A grim smile touched his lips. They were doing the first smart thing they had done. They were moving toward him in unison as they spread out, obviously using a prearranged count for each move forward. He counted off to four between each rustle of the brush and smiled again. They figured to reach him at the same moment and catch him in a cross fire.

Fargo rose, holstered the big Colt, reached up, and grasped the lowest branch with both hands. He pulled himself up, swung long legs over the branch, and sat very still for a long moment. The two men below were still moving carefully forward, one on each side of the tree. Fargo pulled himself up onto one more branch, shifted position, and drew the big Colt again. He could see the two men below, crawling on hands and knees through the brush, almost abreast of the trees. The Trailsman waited, let them reach the tree, and watched as they moved around to the front of the trunk, halted, and half-rose to pour a double volley of shots into the area just behind the base of the tree. He'd have been riddled, Fargo knew, had he still been there.

The two men finished their fusillades, dropped down, and reloaded quickly as they waited and listened. Fargo watched as they cautiously rose. "I think we got him," one called out.

"Wrong," Fargo answered from the tree as he fired. The bullet tore into the nearest man just alongside his neck, traveled downward through his body, and came out at the front of his chest. The man shivered violently for a long moment before he collapsed to the ground. Fargo saw the other one whirl, frown up into the tree as he took desperate seconds trying to find his foe amid the branches. "Drop the gun," Fargo said, but the man followed the sound of his voice, tried bringing his gun around. Fargo fired. The shot hurtled downward into the man's upper chest and drove him into the ground as his legs buckled and he collapsed in an instant pool of red.

Fargo climbed from the tree, holstered the Colt, and hurried back to where he'd left the man with the lariat. He heard the man's groaned curse as he reached the spot and took hold of the rope and yanked the man to his feet. A fleshy-faced figure, the man blinked, became conscious, and stared at the big, black-haired man in front of him. "You're the only one left," Fargo said. "Talk to me."

"I don't know anything," the man muttered sullenly.

"You know who hired you," Fargo snapped.

"I wasn't there," the man said.

Fargo yanked hard on the lariat and the man sprawled forward at his feet. "I don't have time and I don't have patience," Fargo said.

"All right, all right," the man said, and Fargo relaxed his grip on the rope. The man's fleshy face shook as he pushed to his knees. "I've got his name on a piece of paper in here," he said as he reached inside his shirt, felt around with his hand for a moment. "Here it is," he said, began to draw his hand out, and suddenly exploded with an upward lunge, a short, clasp dagger with a buffalo-horn grip in his hand.

Fargo pulled back as the upward slash barely missed

his throat; he stumbled and felt himself fall. He hit the ground, had time only to get his arms up as the man pounced at him with the short-bladed dagger upraised. Fargo managed to close his hand around the man's knife wrist, and the downward thrust of the blade stopped inches from his face. Fargo drew on the powerful muscles of his upper arms and shoulders as he slowly forced the man back, pushed him up, and with a sudden surge of power flipped the fleshy-faced figure away.

The man landed on his side, half-rolled, and slashed out with the short dagger. Again Fargo had to pull back—his legs, this time—as the knife missed only by inches. With surprising speed, the man slashed again as he dived forward, and Fargo had to twist away. He didn't turn back this time, but let himself spin to the side to put more space between himself and the slashing blade. When he halted and turned, the man was charging at him again, his fleshy face twisted into a lumpy snarl. The loose end of the lariat still around his chest whipped wildly in the air as the man dived forward, the dagger raised high.

Fargo held his ground, his lips a thin line, measured split seconds, and dropped to one knee just as the flying figure reached him with the knife. He felt the blade slice the air just over his head as he dropped and lifted a tremendous blow that smashed into the man's midsection. It knocked the figure sideways in midair, and Fargo leapt up as the man hit the ground. He reached out, grasped the loose end of the lariat, yanked hard, and the man hit the ground again as he started to get up.

Fargo moved quickly, sent the rope in a quick loop, and curled it around the man's neck. He let the man half-rise, then he yanked hard on the rope and saw the man's head swivel, his eyes virtually pop from his face. The dagger dropped from his hand as he fell to the ground, his body pointed one way, his head another. Fargo heard the hideous rattling sound that escaped the man's lips, and he relaxed his hold on the rope. The sound stopped and the man stared upward with eyes that would never see again.

"Stupid ass," Fargo muttered as he pulled the lariat free. He went through the man's pockets, found nothing that revealed anything. The others offered no more. He rose, whistled, and the Ovaro came through the trees toward him. He climbed onto the horse and rode south again through the trees until he emerged onto a sunlit path that led between two low hills. The attack rode with him as a shadow he couldn't shake away. Someone didn't want him to reach his destination, and the letter in his jacket pocket had suddenly taken on new dimensions. He drew to a halt at a stream that ran downhill, and dismounted as the horse thirstily drank in the cold, clear water.

Fargo sat down atop a half-rotted log, took the letter from his pocket, unfolded it, and began to read it once again.

Dear Skye Fargo,
    I hope you remember me. It was eight years ago when I last saw you and I was only ten, then. I'm writing for Captain Billy, though he didn't want me to write you. But he is in trouble. There is something very strange going on at the boat and you were the only one I could think of who might be able to help.
    Ten miles west of White Pines there are two hills next to each other. Take the one with a heavy

stand of red oak. Cross to the middle and then go down to the bottom. You'll find an old cabin, I'll wait for you there. Please come.

Caroline Hopkins

Fargo closed the letter and returned it to his pocket. It held nothing he had missed, and he found himself thinking again of Captain Billy as he rose, climbed onto the Ovaro, and rode slowly southward. Captain Billy skippered one of the great riverboats that sailed the Mississippi. Fargo remembered how the captain and his father had been great friends. Captain Billy, a frequent visitor during his stopovers along the great waterway, had almost become a member of the family, and when the letter had come, Fargo knew he'd answer. The letter had reached him care of General Delivery in Austin in Minnesota, where he'd trailblazed for a large herd from North Dakota.

Caroline had obviously found out he was expected there, hardly a secret, and the letter had been there for over a week when he arrived. He half-smiled as his thoughts drifted back to Caroline, Captain Billy's niece. She'd be a grown woman now, eighteen-plus years. He wondered if he'd recognize her, what with the way youngsters changed as they grew, especially females. But the attack had given an urgency to the letter and he put the horse into a trot as he continued to ride south. Another hour had passed when the two hills appeared, almost joined at their bases.

He rode closer, found the one covered with the heavy stand of red oak, and started up the face of the hill. A glance at the sky told him there wasn't much more than an hour of daylight left. He rode across the hill, reached the center, and began to make his way downward through the red oak. He had almost come to the bottom when he spotted the cabin tucked into a small clearing. He turned the Ovaro toward it and reined to a halt as he reached the small open clearing at the face of it.

The door of the cabin opened and a young woman hurried out to meet him as he dismounted, her face wreathed in excitement. "Fargo," she breathed, and was against him, arms around his shoulders in a spontaneous embrace. When she stepped back, he took in an attractive young woman, taller and thinner than he'd expected, the brown hair and brown eyes the same, of course, but her face grown thinner, her pug nose now straighter.

"You've changed," he said.

"It's called growing up," Caroline said.

"Guess so." Fargo smiled. He saw that Caroline wore a thin blouse that outlined somewhat long breasts with full cups that pressed against the fabric with unmistakable points. The compact, firm body he'd known as a ten-year-old had become long and thin, with narrow hips wrapped in a brown skirt short enough to reveal nicely curved calves. She had not only grown up in face and form but had taken on a kind of simmering sensuousness that sent out its own waves.

"Unsaddle your horse and come inside," Caroline said. She waited while he did so, then carried his bedroll inside as dusk began to slide into darkness. She turned on a small lantern and he took in a sparsely furnished cabin with a low wide mattress on a wooden stand to one side, a small fireplace, and a single chair. A row of short wood shelves held an array of assorted trenchers and pots and pans. Caroline sat down on the edge of the mattress, her longish breasts pressed against the thin fabric of the blouse.

"Tell me what this is all about. Your letter didn't say much," Fargo remarked.

"I just want to look at you for a minute," Caroline said. "I think you've grown even handsomer."

"Did you think about a man being handsome eight years ago?" He laughed.

"Of course," she said, and rose and came to him, her hands lifting to press against his face. "Thanks for coming," she said, and he felt the womanly warmth of her. "Captain Billy's in trouble. But he made me promise to let him tell you all about it himself."

"Where is he?"

"On the boat, of course. He can't get away these days. That's why I arranged to meet you here. I've been waiting here most of the week. Captain Billy will be starting back downriver tomorrow. We'll go to meet him," Caroline said.

"He still skipper the *Shady Lady*?"

"That's his boat. He wouldn't skipper any other," Caroline said. She went to an earthenware jar on one of the shelves. "I imagine you're hungry. I've some cold spiced chicken here. It's real good."

"Sounds fine," Fargo said.

"And some good whiskey."

"Sounds even better." He watched her narrow body move with easy grace as she took down two trenchers, the longish breasts swaying with gentle provocativeness. She had indeed grown up, he commented silently, with the kind of tall narrowness he'd never expected. She dished out the chicken and handed him a tin cup for the whiskey she poured from a jar. The night folded itself around the cabin as he began to eat. The whiskey was good, a perfect complement to the spiced chicken, and Caroline nibbled along with him.

"Five dry-gulchers followed me most of the day and finally tried to put me away," he told her. "You have any idea who, why, or what?"

Caroline stared openmouthed at him. "My God," she breathed. "No, I don't. Maybe Captain Billy will." She watched him finish the meal and slowly sip the last of the whiskey. "I don't even want to think about it," she said, and his brows lifted.

"But you sent for me," he said.

"Yes, but there'll be plenty of time tomorrow to talk more about it. I'm just glad you arrived now, so's we can have the night to ourselves," she said.

He felt his brows lift again. "To ourselves?"

"Well, it's turned out this way, and I'm glad," Caroline said, and he saw a soft, dreamy smile come over her face. "I've thought about you all these years, Fargo," she said. "I guess I had a crush on you when I was little that I've never gotten over. I often heard about you over the years. On a riverboat you hear just about everything. Your name came up often, and often by lady passengers."

Fargo shrugged. "Don't believe everything you hear."

"But I did," Caroline said, and the dreamy smile came to her face again. "I had this private dream for years, about my taking the place of those other ladies, about you and me being together. And now we are, even if it's just for a night. It's kind of a dream come true." She halted, tossed an elfin smile at him. "Surprised?" she asked.

"I guess so," he admitted.

"Disappointed?"

"I didn't say that," he answered hastily.

"Good," Caroline said. "Because I believe in making the most of dreams that come true." Her hand went to the thin blouse, pulled open buttons in one quick motion, and with a shrug of her shoulders, the blouse fell from her. She smiled at the appreciation in his eyes as he took in the long curve of her breasts, the full cups swaying as she moved, each a soft white and each tipped by a surprisingly large pink-brown nipple on a circle of matching shade. She stood up, whipped her skirt away, her half-slip with it, to stand before him in lovely nakedness; narrow-hipped, her torso long, her belly flat, almost concave, and a very unruly black triangle pointing down to long legs.

"You have grown up," he said.

"I'll show you how much," Caroline said, and reached out and pulled him to her. She pressed her soft, tall nakedness against him and he felt the warmth of her through his shirt. Her lips found his, an eager, hungry touch. Surprise still pushed at him, he realized. But she wanted to make the most of a dream come true, and he believed in making the most of the unexpected. Surprises were like apples, he reflected as he began to shed clothes. Some were a damn sight sweeter than others.

2

He let his gun belt slide to the floor, clothes follow, and there was nothing between him and her nakedness. She was warm, skin smooth, tingling with the fire of anticipation, and she fell back on the mattress with him. Half over her, he felt her hands at the back of his neck, pressing his face down to her breasts as she twisted, rubbing the soft cream mounds back and forth across his lips. She paused, finally, pushed one firm pink brown tip upward, and he pressed his lips to it, pulling it gently and drawing it upward. Caroline half-screamed in pleasure. "Oh, yes, yes . . . oh, yes," she murmured as he drew the firm tip into his mouth, sucked on it, turned his tongue around its softly firm edges. Caroline's legs rose, came against his sides, pressed, fell away, and pressed again as her body twisted under him.

She pushed up, flesh urging flesh, and her hands pressed into his back. He let one hand move slowly down her long, thin form, paused at the tiny indentation, circled it, and went on, still softly kneading her breast with his lips. Caroline uttered soft sounds of pleasure that suddenly took on strength as his fingers pushed onto the unruly black triangle, pressed against the small rise of flesh under it. One of her hands suddenly moved down his body, searching, probing. She found him, closed her fingers around his pulsating warmth, and her short half-scream of delight came at once. "Oh, Jesus . . . oh, yes," Caroline murmured as she pulled gently on him and he heard his own groan of pleasure.

He felt her legs fall open again and her torso move under him, the body making its own cries, soft, whispered sounds falling from her lips. He felt the unruly triangle push hard against him, the lower part suddenly moist.

"Oh, God, take me . . . Jesus, take me," she murmured. Again she thrust hard against him. He brought his surging desire to the entranceway, touched, and rested. Caroline screamed, a mixture of pleasure and impatience. "No, dammit . . . don't stop," she gasped out.

He moved forward, hardly a half-inch, enough to have the moistness of her encircle him and his throbbing pulse against the aqueous lips. Caroline moaned, demand and desire in the sound, and he felt the quivering of her unruly black triangle. Her legs fell open, her hips lifted, the portal welcoming the visitor, and as he slid forward, he heard the long, gasped groan rise from deep inside her. Her legs closed around him and her warm wetness engulfed, clung, and he felt the pleasure of shared ecstasy. She began to thrust and push at once, moving with his motion. Her hands were against his back, pushing hard. There was no hesitancy, no waiting with her, and he found himself swept along by her eager wanting. Once again, she was a surprise, her unsubtle, almost crude wanting immensely exciting, yet not at all what he expected. He felt himself swept up in her groaning, grunting sounds, each one an exclamation point to their mutual thrusts. His lips found her breasts again and she held him there as she surged against him.

"Yes, yes . . . more, oh, God more," Caroline cried out, and trembled. She seemed about to come but managed to hold back, once, then again, drawing the most from the sweet contact of the senses, the fire of flesh, and the cyclone of wanting. When her sounds finally turned from guttural groans to spiraling screams, he felt her legs stiffen against him and she gave a last feverish convulsion of desire before her screams broke off and she fell back, the longish breasts heaving with her gasped breaths.

Spent, he fell half across her and drew in his own deep breath. She had been thoroughly exciting in her surprisingly unvarnished way, and he turned on one elbow and studied her face and saw the tiny smile edge her lips.

"Great," she murmured, aware of his eyes on her, and she turned, one breast sliding along his chest.

"You do all this growing up on the *Shady Lady*?" Fargo asked idly.

"Some there. Some other places," Caroline said. She stretched, sighed, and he again found himself thinking how he'd never have expected the energetic, feisty little girl he'd known to become such a languorous kitten. She turned on her stomach and he found one of his hands clasping half of her firm, somewhat flat rear as she pushed herself atop him.

"Does Captain Billy know you've grown up so?" Fargo asked.

"I think so," she said. "But I don't want to talk about him now. I don't want to talk."

"What do you want to do?" Fargo questioned.

"More of the same. This might be my one and only chance with you."

"Making the most of dreams come true?"

"Why not?" she shrugged, moved up farther, and lowered one breast to his mouth, pressing the firm brown-pink tip against his lips.

"Why not?" he echoed, and let his lips open. She lowered the soft mound deeper into his mouth. She moaned in delight as his lips curled around her, pulled gently, and he felt her hand moving down his body, again seeking, finding, and quickly closing around him. He responded to her touch at once and Caroline uttered a half-laugh, half-gasp of pleasure. She pressed, stroked, enjoyed the sensation of his burgeoning strength, and suddenly she was half over him, her mouth on his, pressing, wanting, hungering. He felt himself grow anxious again, the tide of desire quickly sweeping through him, and he turned with her as she still clung to him.

But suddenly she pulled back and drew away. "The night chill seeps into this place. I'll light a fire," she said as she swung from the bed.

"We can stay under the sheets," he returned.

"I hate that. I'll only be a minute."

He rose onto one elbow, still pulsating as he waited and watched her stoop down in front of the small fireplace, absolutely at ease in her naked loveliness. She lighted the few logs already there, rose, and came back to him, long-waisted grace in her movements while, behind her, the sparks instantly shot upward into the low chimney. She threw herself onto him as she returned to the bed, pressed hard against him, rubbed her damp triangle against his erectness, and then, arms encircling his neck, flung herself onto her back and pulled him with her. She pushed her pelvis upward, offering again, and once more he let himself enter the welcoming warmth of her. Not as moist now, he noticed abstractly, and her movements less wild. She surged up and down with him but more slowly, a strange deliberateness replacing the urgent fury of the first time. Even her moans were softer and less fervent.

But she gave pleasure, moving smoothly with him, and he was thoroughly caught up in the wondrous ecstasy of the flesh made supreme. Her arms came up, circled his neck, and pulled his face down to her breasts even as she surged against him. His head was cradled between both her breasts and he heard his own groan of pleasure as he moved inside her, the world a wide mattress in a little cabin. He felt himself blink twice, reject the intrusion, take a moment to define the sound: the door had slammed open. Fargo drew his head from her breasts as the voice, harsh and grating, shattered the solitary world.

"That's all, lover," he heard the voice say as he pushed up on his palms, pulled from the young woman, and half-turned to see the four men there, two already in the room, two still in the doorway, all with guns in hand. He sank down on his haunches on the mattress as one of the men scooped his gun belt from the floor. "Get up," the one man ordered, a sneer on his wide, heavily stubbled face.

Fargo rose from his haunches and swung from the bed, aware he was still aroused and feeling nakedly helpless. He glanced at Caroline and saw her push from the bed with almost casual deliberateness. He felt the frown touch his brow as she looked at the four men with not a touch of surprise in her face—not a touch of modesty, either, he noted idly.

"You took long enough, girlie," the stubble-faced one muttered.

"I had to wait. I wanted to make sure he was really relaxed," she said, and calmly drew on skirt and blouse.

Fargo's thoughts whirled, one spiraling through all the others, exploding inside him with a shower of bitterness. "You're not Caroline," he breathed.

"Bull's-eye," the young woman said. "I'm not Caroline."

"Who the hell are you?" he bit out.

"Hired help. Aggie, if you want a name. Somebody paid me to do a job," she said.

Fargo bent over, scooped his trousers up, and put them on as the young woman regarded him with calm unconcern. "What happened to Caroline?" he asked.

"Don't know. She never showed. I expected she would, but she didn't," Aggie said.

The stubble-faced man interrupted. "We thought you forgot about the signal, honey," he said.

"I told you. I had to make sure he was relaxed," she answered with a show of annoyance.

"Lighting the fire was the signal, wasn't it?" Fargo put in.

"Two in a row," Aggie said mockingly, and now there was only hardness in her face.

"You did your job well," Fargo said.

"I enjoyed it. You were real good," she said with a kind of clinical detachment.

Fargo cursed under his breath. She was so instantly changed, and now all the little things flooded back. She'd taken her cues from things he had said, given

27

answers that were just enough and yet deft sidesteps. Her experienced ways had surprised him, the manner in which she had taken charge, edged crudeness, set the wheels into motion, and guided the pace of things. It was all so clear now, new light shedding knowledge. But, then, it was always easy to see afterward.

"What happens now?" Fargo asked as he drew on clothes.

"It's only a few hours till daylight. We stay here and then take you to our boss," the wide-faced one said, plainly the leader of the four.

"What's he want with me?" Fargo asked.

"He wants to know what you know," the man answered, and gestured to his companions. "Tie him up," he ordered, and Fargo's glance went to the six-gun trained on him. There was no way the man could miss at such close range, he decided. He brought his wrists out in front of him as the two men approached. They bound his wrists together with a length of lariat and stepped back. But they had responded to his gesture and left his wrists tied in front of him. He smiled inwardly at their inept stupidity. He was pushed to the floor in a corner of the room and one of the men stood guard over him.

"I'm not waiting for morning. My horse is tied in back. I'm cutting out now," the young woman said.

"Who hired you?" Fargo asked.

"A man," she said, and picked up a small canvas bag as she strode from the cabin and slammed the door shut. Minutes later, the sound of her horse trotting away drifted into the cabin.

"We'll take turns watching him," the stubble-faced man said. "You first, Elwood." One of the others sat down opposite him, six-gun in hand, Fargo saw, while the wide-faced spokesman for the group stretched out on the mattress and the other two lay down on the floor.

Fargo grimaced as he thought about the girl. She had been smooth, he reflected. She had deflected talking about Captain Billy, her few answers really just following statements he had made, other replies clever evasions. But she had known the real Caroline hadn't seen him since she was a little girl. She had been coached on that. Someone had known enough to tell her that. Or had drawn it out of Caroline . . . He grimaced at the thought. Somebody felt it very important that he not meet with the real Caroline Hopkins. Important enough to go to elaborate lengths, to kill for it. Fargo frowned. That meant there was much more than Caroline's letter to him had implied.

He pushed away thoughts and glanced at the man guarding him. Bound as he was, Fargo realized, he could do nothing here in the cabin. He put his head back against the wall and closed his eyes. He had learned long ago to make the best of a bad situation, and sometimes that meant nothing more than biding one's time. He relaxed, let sleep come to him, woke as the men changed guards, and quickly returned to sleep.

When day filtered into the cabin, Fargo was awake. He watched the others rise, step outside, and motion for him to follow. They gave him a few minutes to freshen up as best he could with his wrists tied, and they kept a guard on him who walked behind him as he strode to the Ovaro and pulled himself into the saddle. "How long do we ride?" he queried.

"A day maybe. Won't make much difference to you. You're vulture meat when the boss gets through with you," the wide-faced one said.

"Much obliged," Fargo grunted, but he had his answer. He'd have the better part of a day to find a moment, a spot, a chance to make his move. They weren't the kind to stay alert for long. There would be a moment, and he could only hope that the terrain was right for it when it came.

The wide-faced man rode in front of Fargo, the other two flanking him on both sides, and the fourth rode close behind. The Trailsman held the saddle horn with both hands, flexed his arm muscles, and found the wrist ropes had some slack in them. But the important thing was that his hands were in front of him, not behind his back, and he rode casually as the stubble-faced one set an even pace.

They headed west, he took note, and as the morning wore on, he saw his captors relax under the hot sun. The one behind him had dropped a half-dozen paces back and the two on each side of him had drifted in too close to him. He grunted silently and swept the terrain with his eyes, saw it grow into a succession of low hills thick with box elder and scarlet haw. The man in front led the way along a narrow passage at the base of two hills, hardly wide enough for two horses abreast, and one of the men at his side dropped back to follow single-file.

Fargo's eyes flicked from one side of the narrow path to the other. There was enough dense brush, but it was too even across the ground. They'd catch him in minutes. He needed someplace that held a drop-off or a gulley, a place to give him enough time to work on the wrist bonds. He grimaced and abandoned the idea of making a move at this spot. He turned the Ovaro to follow the stubble-faced man as he took another path north.

The heavily foliaged hills still rose up on both sides, and they had gone on for perhaps another hour when the air exploded with a rifle shot, the sound bouncing from the hills to make it sound not unlike a small cannon. Fargo saw the man at his right topple from his horse as though a giant, invisible hand had swept him away. The others halted, wheeled, peered up into the trees in confusion, and a second shot rang out. Another of the men flew out of the saddle, this time with his chest gushing a stream of red.

Fargo swung one leg over the saddle and leapt to the ground, glimpsed the other two men doing the same as a third shot missed. He landed on the balls of his feet, dived, rolled into the thick brush, and came up on his stomach. He stayed down and saw the stubble-faced man, six-gun in hand, a half-dozen yards to his left. The man crouched, peering into the hills. Fargo glanced to his left to see the other man in the brush, his eyes also scanning the slopes.

The two men weren't thinking about him now, all their concentration on the unseen assailant. A sudden flash of movement halfway up the hill brought both men to their feet and firing. Fargo saw the horse and rider come into view, move to the left across the hill, and disappear just as quickly into the trees again. But the stubble-faced man ran to his left, still firing, and Fargo watched the second man start to cross in front of him. He rose to a crouch, moved forward as the man reached him, his concentration on the hillside.

Fargo swung with both arms, his bound wrists together. The blow, awkward but powerful, slammed into the man's back and sent him falling forward with a grunt of pain. The gun fell from the man's hand, and

Fargo dived, pounced on it with both hands, whirled onto his back, the gun held in front of him. The man, on his feet, aimed a kick at him, but Fargo twisted to one side, swung the gun around again, still holding it with both hands. He fired at the charging figure and the bullet hurtled into the man at close range. The man halted as though he'd run into an invisible wall, quivered in place for a moment as his midsection became an uneven red blotch, and then collapsed to the ground.

But the stubble-faced man had whirled. Fargo heard his shot, felt the bullet graze his head. He rolled, rolled again as another bullet kicked up the ground inches from him. He had to twist and roll again to avoid still another shot when the heavy sound of the rifle exploded. Fargo turned, glanced up, to see the man stumble, then pitch faceforward to the ground. Silence descended at once and Fargo stayed in the brush as he called out. "It's over," he shouted. "They're all dead. You can come down, whoever you are."

He waited, his eyes sweeping the hillside and suddenly the horse and rider appeared again, moved from the foliage and began to walk downhill. He saw the rider, a figure in a jacket with an upturned collar and a wide-brimmed stetson, put the rifle into a saddle holster and he rose to his feet. The rider immediately turned the horse toward him, reached the bottom of the hill and reined to a halt in front of him. Fargo watched the figure reach up, take the hat off and felt his jaw drop open as he saw brown hair, cut short and pulled back in a pony tail that bounced from side to side. "I'll be damned," he muttered as the young woman swung to the ground with a quick, bouncy motion.

He realized he was staring as he took in a young, smooth face, pretty and pugnacious at the same time, snapping brown eyes, round cheeks, a short turned-up nose, and full lips. It was a face from yesterday, grown up now, fuller, stronger, yet not all that much changed, the feistiness still very much a part of it, and he cursed himself for the rationalizations he had used only the day before. "Caroline," he said, no question in the word this time.

"That's right," the girl said firmly, and took off the jacket with its upturned collar. "I won't be needing that anymore, either."

"You want to put all this together for me?" Fargo asked.

"Not here. Let's ride," she said.

"Soon as I get these ropes off," Fargo answered, and held up his bound wrists. "There's a knife in an ankle holster on my right leg. It'll be quicker if you cut them."

The young woman reached down, pulled his trouser leg up, and drew the thin, double-edged throwing knife from the calf holster. She cut the ropes with two quick slices of the knife and handed the blade back to him. He took another moment to retrieve his Colt from the lifeless form nearby and turned to climb onto the Ovaro.

Caroline pulled herself into the saddle, a compact, short figure, Levi's tight against a round, firm rear and a tan shirt that lay atop very round, very high breasts. He followed her as she took a path that led east. They rode in silence until she came to a small, spring-fed pond and dismounted. She moved with an energetic kind of grace, the round, high breasts moving in uni-

33

son, he noted. But he frowned inwardly at the simmering anger he saw in her face.

"I'll tell you what I can. It's not all that much," Caroline said as she faced him.

"Let's start with the girl in the cabin who posed as you," Fargo said.

"Let's," Caroline said, and he frowned again at the testiness in her voice. "Only I don't know anything at all about her."

"Somebody sent her there, hired her for it. You must have realized that."

"Not until it was too late to do anything about it."

"Suppose you start at the beginning."

"I'll start from when I sent you the letter," she said firmly. "That's when this part begins. I sent it when the boat stopped at Wyalusing. It's a town with not much of a mail depot, but it was all that there was. We had an unexpected delay at Wyalusing. One of the paddle wheels had jammed, so we stayed over an extra day. I stopped by at the mail depot to make sure the letter had gone out. The man at the depot told me that my brother had come looking for the letter. My brother, he said, told him I'd changed my mind about sending it."

"Only you don't have a brother," Fargo said, and she nodded, her lips set grimly.

"Whoever it was was too late. The letter had gone out. But I knew then that somebody was out to stop our meeting."

"Somebody knew about your writing me. That's damn plain." Fargo frowned. "How many people did you tell?"

She made a wry face. "I didn't make a secret of it. I guess a lot of people could have heard."

"Not very smart."

"A mistake," she conceded brusquely. "I'd no idea somebody would try to stop me from meeting you."

"Somebody tried. Twice."

"After I realized something was going on, I didn't know exactly what to do. It was too late to reach you again by mail, and I knew I could never cover all the different ways you might come."

"So you decided to watch the cabin," Fargo said. "That seems the first smart thing you did."

Caroline tossed him a quick glare. "I found a place on top of the hill where I could hide and see the cabin. I was afraid to wait there for you myself, not knowing who might show up. I saw the girl arrive in a few days, a man with her, but he left right away. I stayed hidden and watched. It was all I could do. Then, a day after, the four men came and settled in near the top of the hill. It was plain they were watching the cabin, too."

"And finally I showed up," Fargo said.

"That's right. I couldn't go down to warn you. I could only wait and watch. When the four men finally moved down to the cabin to surprise you, I knew I'd have to wait for a better place and time to hit them," Caroline said. "As for the girl, I knew she was going to impersonate me."

"Which is exactly what she did."

"And you fell for it," Caroline sniffed.

"I hadn't seen you since you were a little girl. People change when they grow up, especially females," he said with more defensiveness than he had intended.

"It was plain she did more than talk about old times," Caroline said disdainfully. "She made sure you were very much preoccupied when those four came down to interrupt you."

"That was their plan, obviously. She was part of it," Fargo admitted. "She played her part well."

"And you were so quick to oblige," Caroline snapped, anger and reproof in her voice.

He studied her for a moment. "Is that what's been digging at you?" he asked with a half-smile.

"Maybe."

"Why?"

"You slept with me. I mean, you thought it was me," Caroline tossed back, brown eyes snapping.

"Something wrong in that?" he slid at her.

"There most certainly is."

"You sorry it wasn't really you?" he remarked, and received a glare.

"I certainly am not!"

"Then what's the matter?"

"I think sleeping with someone you held on your knee only eight years ago is somehow wrong," Caroline threw back.

"Why?" he asked blandly.

"I don't know why, it just is," she half-shouted in exasperation.

"Not to me," Fargo said. "Aren't you the prim and proper one."

"I'm not prim and proper."

"I used to live near a young tree once. Thin branches, only a few leaves, not enough shade for an ant. When I left, it grew quickly. Next time I saw it it was a fine grown tree with lots of branches and lots of leaves. I didn't see anything wrong in sleeping under it because I knew it when it was young and skinny," Fargo said.

"It's not the same. Girls are not trees."

"They grow. They blossom. It's not so different,"

Fargo remarked. She dismissed the answer with a sniff and strode to the horse.

"Let's ride," she said, and he climbed onto the Ovaro.

"So much for what happened for now. Tell me why you sent for me in the first place," Fargo said, and swung beside her as she took another passage eastward. "Tell me about Captain Billy and the *Shady Lady*."

"The boat has been raided regularly by Indians," Caroline said. "Too regularly."

"Indian raids on riverboats are nothing new. Neither are raids by river pirates," Fargo said.

"Yes, true enough, but these Indians haven't done the usual: held up passengers or the crew, robbed them of watches and trinkets. These carried off bags of wheat and grain shipments in their canoes."

"That *is* strange," Fargo said as his brows knitted. "Indians making off with wheat and grain shipments. Doesn't figure."

"They did kill a few passengers and crewmen who tried to stop one of the raids," Caroline said.

"I don't see this needing a trailsman."

"We'll need the shipments tracked. That's where you come in. We have to get them back. Captain Billy is responsible for those shipments while they're on his boat. He'll have to make up the loss. It could be enough to ruin him," she said.

"You wrote that he didn't want to send for me. Why?" Fargo asked.

"He's discouraged. He's grown old. He's not the man you used to know. He felt that he'd no right to ask your help and that we'd only be wasting your time," she answered.

"You felt differently."

"Obviously," she sniffed, and he smiled. The feistiness of the little girl he'd known was very much part of the young woman. "Friends are for calling on when you need them. He often talked about your father. They were good friends. And about you, too." She halted and her lips tightened. "Besides, I didn't know where else to turn," she added.

"The *Shady Lady* still have the big gaming salon?" Fargo asked.

"It sure does. That brings in more money than passengers or freight. You see, Captain Billy has the poor part of the run," Caroline said.

"Meaning what?"

"He only goes from St. Louis north to the headwaters and back. The real money routes are the boats that go south from St. Louis, downriver to New Orleans."

"Why can't he do that?"

"You can't go onto somebody else's route and the big side-wheelers like the *Delta Queen* and the *Cotton Queen* have those routes," Caroline explained. "Not that the *Shady Lady* couldn't make big-enough profits."

"Why doesn't it?" Fargo questioned.

"Captain Billy has a lot of old customers he keeps at the old low rates. That and his own gambling ways when we hit St. Louis. That's why he can't pay off those losses."

"You're part of the boat. What part?"

"I keep the books for Captain Billy. That's how I know how little he clears and how much he gambles away. That's why I know we have to get back those grain shipments. He can't stand taking those losses."

Fargo fell silent and rode with thoughts moving through his head like tumbleweed. The crease stayed on his brow as he rode beside Caroline. "It doesn't fit," he said suddenly, and she glanced at him with her own brow furrowed. "There's got to be more, something worth killing for."

"Such as?"

"Somebody tried to have me killed so we wouldn't meet. Just because I might track some Indians stealing grain shipments? It doesn't make sense. I'm thinking they might even be fake Indians," Fargo said, and Caroline continued to frown at him. "You said Captain Billy can't stand paying the losses on these raided shipments. Maybe that's what's behind it: somebody out to see that he goes under."

"Why?"

"To take over the boat. You said it could make real money, run right," Fargo suggested.

Caroline's brown eyes became small saucers and her lips fell open. "I never thought of that." She gasped.

"If I stopped the raids and tracked down the shipments stolen so far, that would wreck the scheme. That'd be worth killing for," Fargo said, warming to the thought.

"Yes, it would," Caroline breathed.

"It's just a thought, but it makes some of the pieces fit," Fargo mused aloud. "There'd be no sense in killing to stop me from tracking down some Indian raiders."

"No, I guess not," Caroline said. "And it'd explain the raids, which don't make any damn sense on their own."

Fargo nodded and glanced up at the sky where the

late-day clouds were beginning to slide across the horizon. "Where are we going?"

"The *Shady Lady* will have turned around at Winona this morning. She'll start back soon after, and we ought to see her late tonight. We'll ride alongside on the shore and board when she docks at Dubuque in the morning," Caroline answered, and continued to lead the way east as night descended. A half-moon rose and she halted at a stream to water and rest her horse. "We can rest some," she said, sliding out of the saddle. "No point in reaching the river too early."

"I've some beef jerky we can share," Fargo said, and she came to sit beside him.

"I'm sorry I was so sharp with you before, about that girl," she murmured. "I'd no right."

"You're sorry, but you still feel the same way." He smiled.

"Yes," she answered firmly. "So she did the pushing but you still thought she was me. Maybe I was carrying out a silly infatuation or just being desperate. You should've thought about that and turned away instead of being so glad to hop into bed with me. That would've been the gentlemanly thing to do."

"I'll try to remember that," Fargo said, and watched as she sat back on her elbows, her face turned up to the silver light of the moon, the very round, high breasts pressed tight against the shirt. In the moonlight, her round-cheeked, snub-nosed face, framed by the short hair and ponytail, seemed hardly changed from when she was a little girl.

She felt his eyes on her, lowered her head, and glanced at him. "What are you thinking?"

"How much the little girl is still in your face," he said.

"But not in the rest of me?"

"Definitely not."

"It's called growing up," she said.

"Outside if not inside," he remarked, and received a quick glare.

"We'll rest for an hour and then go on," she said, firmly changing the subject, and he smiled as he closed his eyes.

3

"We're here, all three of us. Even with your directions it was hard enough finding this abandoned shack."

"We've each come alone. I understand you've questions, Fullerton. Ask them now. This will be our only meeting. None of us can risk another, particularly Lord Upshaw."

"That's right. Her majesty's government cannot appear to be involved in any way."

The third man's thick, bushy brows formed a frown. "I understand that, but I thought you were only representing the Import Shippers' Association."

"True, but I'm also her majesty's minister of trade. We can't afford even the slightest appearance of wrong. Washington is suspicious enough as it is."

"What are your questions, Fullerton?"

"About the shipments. Only two shipments were received, but the boat has made eight stops at St. Louis. My people were waiting each time, but there was no signal and nothing came through except for the first two times."

"Then we must assume there were no shipments. Our shipments may well be highly erratic. They are being sent through very complicated channels. A certain amount of irregularity must be expected."

"Our operative on the riverboat is the only one who knows whether a shipment is actually on board, and can give the right signal at the right time. But even our agent doesn't know any more than that."

"It's all been carefully arranged that way. Our agent on board is to watch whatever goes on on the riverboat, especially for the presence of federal government agents. Your job, Fullerton, is to receive the shipments, stay back, and turn aside anything unexpected from outside."

"There have been a number of Indian raids on the boat."

"That doesn't concern us. All we care about is that our shipments go through."

"Yes, but I learned that the captain's niece sent for help in stopping the raids, a man named Skye Fargo. He's also called the Trailsman and he has a reputation for nosing around. God knows what he might turn up. He's also worked closely with the army in the past. I decided it'd be best if he never got aboard the boat, just to be on the safe side.

"Then see to it."

"I've done that already."

"Good."

"Then this meeting is over. You know where to contact the emergency forces we've sent up here and our agent on the riverboat knows how to contact you. That should be enough. You just see that our shipments are sent on as planned when they arrive."

"Yes, sir."

The two horses snorted as they stood at the edge of

the shore, hooves almost in the water. The big man on the Ovaro scanned the dark slow-moving river that wound its way south, a seemingly endless watery avenue. Mississippi, the Indians had named it—probably the Chippewa—Father of the Waters. And indeed it was, winding its way through and between a dozen states and territories. It could be peaceful, sweet as the magnolia that lined much of its banks. It could rage and flood and wipe out everything in its path. It could be benevolent, carrying a boat smoothly on gentle currents, and it could be treacherous with shifting sandbars and hidden obstacles. But with all, it was a lifeline for a new nation, reaching from the headwaters of Lake Itasca in Minnesota Territory all the way down to the Gulf Coast port of New Orleans, changing character all along its way. Those who traveled its circuitous path were a cross section of the new nation—settlers sailing north in their arks that often looked more like a farmyard than a boat, merchants with their keel boats loaded with dry goods and dresses, pioneers, dreamers, wanderers, and idlers.

The great riverboats carried anyone with the price of a ticket: fire-and-brimstone preachers and fancy ladies, slave-holders and abolitionists, men of law and men without law, those going someplace and those going noplace. Some were wide-beamed side-wheelers and some were stern-wheelers, but all were the queens of the Mississippi, each endowed with its own stately beauty, sometimes looking perfect against the graceful willows on the great banks, sometimes looking as misplaced as a dowager in a dance hall.

Fargo's lake-blue eyes peered north to where the river rounded a short bend. He heard the boat before he saw it—the deep, throbbing sound of the great paddle wheel drifting through the night. Moments later, the riverboat came into view, ghostly white in the moonlight, only the main salon still lighted. A shower of sparks and smoke rose from the filigreed tops of the two tall, parallel smokestacks while a white plume drifted skyward from the tall steam funnel amidships.

Fargo's eyes followed the *Shady Lady* as it moved slowly past, and he backed the Ovaro from the edge of the water. "Let's ride," he murmured to Caroline.

"We'll just keep pace till she docks at Dubuque, come morning," Caroline said.

"No. I'm going to board tonight." Caroline's frown was instant. "They didn't want us to meet. That means they don't want me aboard, and they could be watching at Dubuque. I want as much time aboard before anyone finds out I'm there."

"How do you expect to get aboard tonight? The boat will stay in midriver all the way."

"Swim. We'll get downriver far enough ahead so's I'll be able to swim out to her. Then you'll take my horse and bring him aboard with you tomorrow," Fargo said. He didn't wait for a reply as he sent the Ovaro into a gallop along the shoreline and left the slow-moving riverboat behind.

He heard Caroline on his heels as he rode a quarter-mile downriver and reined to a halt. He leapt to the ground, rummaged through his saddlebag until he found his rain slicker. As Caroline watched from the saddle, he pulled off his clothes down to his underdrawers and wrapped everything, including his gun belt, in the rain slicker. Finished, he turned to see Caroline's eyes moving across the muscled symmetry of his near-naked

45

body. She pulled her eyes away as she met his glance, and he smiled as he tied the ends of the rain slicker around his waist. The riverboat was approaching out of the dark waters with more speed than he'd expected. He stepped into the river. "See you tomorrow," he called back to Caroline as the shore disappeared from beneath his feet and he began to swim.

The shower of sparks rising from the two tall funnels were as twin beacons as he swam into the river. He found the water both warm and sluggish. As the boat came on, he swam harder, reached midriver, and gauged the dark object's speed. The prow with the wide, curved gunwale—a kind of ledge over the cutting edge—passed close to him. He felt the waves from the boat lift him, trying to turn him around. He paddled harder. He had to move in against the midsection, where the gunwale was hardly more than a foot over the water. Any miscalculation could catch him in the strong undertow of the hull and sweep him into the paddle wheel.

The center section of the boat slid past and Fargo pushed hard against the dark water, reached the boat, and grabbed hold, grateful for the lowness of the gunwales. He curled both hands around the wood strip, clung for a moment, and let himself be dragged along. Getting a firmer grip, he pulled one leg over the low side, followed with the rest of his body, and lay still on the deck for a long minute. When he rose, he took in the cords of wood that were stacked against the side of the boiler-room wall. He sank down, unwrapped the oilskin from around his waist, and set it aside on the wood to dry. He let himself dry out and finally pulled on trousers and sat back. The pilot house, high atop the midsection of the boat, was impossible to see from where he sat. He wondered if Captain Billy was at the wheel. He decided to wait till morning and settled down, his eyes searching the shoreline as the boat slowly moved downriver. He stayed awake for most of what was left of the night, but nothing moved on shore, no furtive figures pushing out from the river banks.

The Trailsman felt the weariness stab at him as day broke. The sun took the dark magic out of the river even as it revealed the waterway in a different kind of splendor. He rose, pulled on his clothes, strapped on his gun belt, and heard the boat come alive with footsteps and voices. The passenger cabins were on the upper decks with their arched and filigree-decorated railings. Like most riverboats, the cargo section was at the waterline along with a small stable for those who wanted to travel with their horses.

He heard the crew start to feed the boilers as he left the cords of wood and climbed the narrow companionway nearby. It rose to the upper decks and the pilot house high over the center of the boat. He paused outside as he saw Captain Billy's unmistakable figure at the wheel, short and stocky of build, a roly-poly shape, his captain's cap worn at a jaunty angle.

Fargo opened the door noiselessly and stepped into the pilot house. "Captain Billy Hopkins, I do believe," he said softly.

The man spun, stared at him openmouthed.

"Fargo. I'll be dammed," the captain said.

Fargo felt himself stare back. Captain Billy's face was still round, the cheeks still full, but the jolly, cherubic look had become something else, a kind of dyspeptic elf. The quick, wide smile had taken on a mechanical air, and little lines turned down the corners of his mouth. The face was now a caricature of itself.

"How did you get aboard?" the captain asked.

"Magic," Fargo said, and gripped the man's outstretched hand.

"By God, it's good to see you," Captain Billy said. "You met with Caroline, I take it."

"I did. She'll be coming aboard at Dubuque as she originally planned. She gave me a fast rundown on what's been going on. It doesn't add up," Fargo said. "Especially seeing as how somebody tried to kill me to stop me from meeting Caroline."

"By God," Captain Billy said, his round face growing sober. "I told Caroline not to involve you in this."

"That doesn't bother me. It's what it means that sets me to wondering," Fargo said. "You get a good look at the Indians who have been doing the raiding?"

"Good as possible in the dark and ducking bullets," the captain said. "Saux Fox, I'd guess. They attack from Saux Fox territory."

"That makes it even stranger. The Fox have been at peace for years." Fargo frowned.

"Any Indian can get unpeaceful," Captain Billy spit out, and Fargo had to concede the truth in his words. He was about to ask further when the pilot-house door opened and a tall, lanky, dour-faced man entered, a ship's officer cap on his head, long, lined creases part of his dour expression, his eyes very dark under beetling brows. "Ez Crawley, my first mate," Captain Billy introduced. "This is Skye Fargo, Ez."

The man's dour face didn't change expression. "You're the one Caroline set out to fetch," he said.

"In person." Fargo smiled, but the man's face remained wooden. "You get a look at the Indians doing the raiding?" Fargo asked the mate.

"No. I'm a first mate, not an Indian fighter. I kept away and saved my neck."

"Take the wheel, Ez," Captain Billy ordered, and led Fargo to the outside deck. "Ez is a good first mate. He's just not a man who's about to stick his neck out."

"There are plenty like him." Fargo shrugged. "Who else knows Caroline sent for me?"

"I'd guess a good part of our regular crew," the captain answered. "Caroline talked enough about it. Any one of them could've told somebody else. Even some of the passengers. We have our regular passengers who ride the *Shady Lady* every week."

"Caroline tells me you can't take the loss of so many shipments," Fargo said. "She says you can't cover the payment."

"Guess she's right enough there," Captain Billy said, his cherubic face somehow growing longer. "Maybe that'll finally make me pack it in."

"You've skippered on the river all your life. You don't know anything else," Fargo protested.

"There comes a time. I'm tired, Fargo. Too much work and nothing much to show for it. The years take their toll."

"So does squandering your money at the gambling joints in St. Louis," Fargo slid back.

Captain Billy's eyes narrowed. "That damn girl always did talk too much."

"Maybe you ought to gamble here on the *Shady Lady*. You'd get back part of your losses in what the house takes."

"Couldn't do that. Hell, every other player would holler about the captain gambling on his own tables," Billy said. "But it all comes out the same way. Forty years of sailing the Mississippi is enough. Of course, I don't want to go out with a huge debt around my neck."

"I think somebody's trying to help you go out, Billy," Fargo said, and quickly outlined what he'd told Caroline.

The captain frowned out across the river when Fargo finished. "By God, I never thought of anything like that."

"It's the only thing that makes the pieces fit. Indians don't naturally go around stealing grain shipments. I'd even guess they're fake Indians. Somebody's out to saddle you with losses you can't pay."

"So I'd have to put the boat up to pay. It's my only asset," the captain murmured, and Fargo saw despair slide into the shock on the man's round face. "That might be exactly what's going to happen. I don't see how even you can track down those shipments."

"I'm here. I'll try my best," Fargo said.

"Well, I sure appreciate that."

"Meanwhile, I could use some sleep."

"We don't have an empty cabin. Use Caroline's. We won't make Dubuque till this afternoon. We're running late," the captain said. "I'll show you the way."

"Good. I want to stay low as long as I can," Fargo said, following Captain Billy down the companionway and onto the middle deck.

The captain halted as a woman came out of one of the side doors. She wore a robe that clung to full

50

breasts and a full-hipped figure. Fargo took in a wide face, more pleasant than pretty, curly brown hair and brown eyes that held a frank, almost challenging expression. A wide mouth added to the sensuousness he felt about her.

"Darlene Binder," Captain Billy introduced. "Darlene waits tables, serves drinks, and acts as a kind of hostess in the gaming room."

"When did you come aboard, handsome?" Darlene asked.

"When you weren't looking," Fargo said, and a tiny furrow touched her brow. "You'll have to keep your eyes open wider," he added.

"I guess so," she murmured, the furrow staying. She was pushing at thirty-five, Fargo guessed, but she was trim, only a few telltale wrinkles at the corner of her eyes. "See you around, big man," she said, and hurried down the corridor.

"Seems right friendly," Fargo remarked.

"Maybe too much so. But she does her job well and she's been discreet. The passengers like her," Billy said.

"How long has she been with you?" Fargo asked.

"Came looking for a job about two months ago," Billy said. "Same time as I hired Monica."

"Monica?"

"Monica Milford. She's our faro dealer, and a damn good one. Now, there's a gal with class and brains," Captain Billy said, halting as they passed a window that looked out on the deck. "You can meet her now." He opened a doorway to the deck before Fargo could stop him. "Monica," Captain Billy called, and Fargo stepped outside to face a tall young woman, a willowy figure even clad in Levi's and a blue checked shirt, with breasts that curved in a long line from the opened top buttons of the shirt. But her face held him, a strikingly beautiful face, jet-black hair that hung low, black-brown eyes, a patrician nose and cleanly etched lips that seemed unusually red against pale-white skin. "This is Skye Fargo, Monica," Billy said, and a smile came to the lovely lips.

"Caroline's savior," the young woman said, her voice low and husky.

"I wouldn't go that far. An old friend is closer to the truth," Fargo said.

"I don't recall seeing you board," Monica Milford said.

"Almost what Darlene said," the captain interjected. "Fargo has his own way of doing things."

"I'm sure," Monica said with an appraising glance and a smile that was both warm and dazzling. "Perhaps I'll see you later this evening, Fargo."

"Perhaps," Fargo said, and returned inside the boat with the captain.

"Great girl, Monica," Captain Billy said. "I'm lucky she showed up when she did. My regular faro dealer went ashore one day and never came back. She made a good pitch for the job and I hired her."

"A case of being at the right spot at the right time, I'd say," Fargo commented.

"For everybody," the captain said. "She's gotten real friendly with a gambling man who's been traveling on the boat. But she's discreet and he doesn't play at her table."

"So much for Monica. Now, tell me, do you have another of those grain shipments aboard now?"

Fargo asked as he walked down the corridor with the captain.

"We do," Captain Billy said.

"Where are they consigned?"

"Fullerton Haulage, an outfit in St. Louis," the captain said.

"Then there's a good chance you could get another raid tonight," Fargo inquired.

"Or tomorrow night. They're clever. It's plain that they watch from inside the shore trees. They wait till we stop in midriver."

"Why would you do that?" Fargo frowned.

"Planters, sawyers, or sleepers," the captain said.

Fargo frowned and pulled at his memory. "They're all names for river obstacles, right?"

"Right. Some are tangled snags of branches. Sometimes they can be whole trees or rotted logs twisted up in thick branches," the captain said. "Planters have one end permanent into the river bottom, but they often reach to the surface. You can usually see them by day but not easily by night. Sawyers rise up and down in their own rhythm. You can never tell when one will rise up right in front of you or, worse yet, come up under the hull to tangle in the paddle wheel. Sleepers are snags that stay just under the surface so you don't see them until you hit them. They're all bad, each in their own way."

"I'll keep watch during the night," Fargo said as the captain halted at a cabin door and pushed it open. The Trailsman saw a small cabin decked out with pink bows, a dresser with powders and perfumes on the top, and a single bed against one wall that suddenly looked terribly inviting. "I've an oilskin slicker on the woodpile. Have somebody fetch it for me?" he asked.

"I'll have one of the cabin boys bring it to the door," the captain said.

"See you tonight," Fargo said as he shut the cabin door, quickly pulled off clothes, and stretched his powerful frame out on the bed. The sheet smelled faintly of bath oil, and he went to sleep thinking pleasant things.

The soft rocking motion of the boat was its own lullaby and he slept heavily, to wake only when he heard the latch on the door come open. He sat up, one hand on the Colt in the holster by his side. The door opened wider and he saw the snub-nosed face push into the room.

Caroline's eyes found him, widened, and he pulled the sheet over his groin. "What are you doing here?" she asked.

"There was no room at the inn. Captain Billy's suggestion," Fargo said, and pushed up to a sitting position as Caroline came in and put her things on a chair.

"I'm exhausted. I've been in the saddle all night and most of today. I need some sleep," Caroline said.

"It's all yours," Fargo said, and swung from the bed. She turned away as he pulled on clothes. "The Ovaro stabled on board?" he asked.

"Yes, with instructions to take special care of him," Caroline said as she turned back. His shirt still off, he sat down on the rug that covered the floor of the cabin and lay back. "What are you doing?" Caroline frowned.

"Staying here till after dark. I'll get in a few more winks, too," Fargo answered. "I want to stay out of sight."

"But you can't!"

"I'm giving you the bed."

"I have to undress."

"I'll close my eyes," he murmured.

"Promise you won't peek," she said, suddenly sounding ten years younger.

He grimaced. "That'd be hard to promise."

"Just as I thought," she sniffed disapprovingly.

"I'll compromise. If I peek, I won't applaud," he said.

She glared back. "I guess everything I've heard about you is true."

"Probably," he agreed mildly, and closed his eyes. He heard her storming about, opened one eye to see her stretch a sheet from the dresser to the bedpost. She disappeared behind it and he closed his eye and listened to her undress and finally take the sheet down. Clothed in a thin, pink nightgown, she was crawling into the bed as he opened his eyes, her round rear pressing the fabric smooth. She lay down with her back to him and he heard her deep sigh of exhaustion.

"You talk to Captain Billy?" she asked.

"I did," Fargo said.

"It'll have to wait till later. I'm too tired to think about anything."

"Then go to sleep," Fargo advised, and closed his eyes to enjoy the additional hours of sleep.

When he woke the cabin was pitch-black, night surrounding the ship. Caroline was sound asleep, her breathing deep and heavy, and he left the cabin on soundless steps. He went out on deck and made his way to the pilot house to find Captain Billy at the wheel.

"Double shift today," Billy said. "Ez went ashore at

55

Dubuque. He had some time off coming to him. He'll rejoin the ship downriver, probably at Moline."

"I'll be doing some nightwork, too," Fargo said. "Though I figure to stay mostly out of sight until there's trouble. The men who tried to kill me knew I was meeting Caroline. Seems to me that somebody on board had to contact them."

"As you know, Caroline didn't keep her plans a secret. But that doesn't mean it was one of my people. A passenger could've overheard. Or the crew talked at a local bar during one of the overnight stops. That happens often enough."

Fargo grimaced at the truth of the captain's words. It expanded the possibilities past calculating. But he had to start someplace, and he'd make it the boat for now. "See you later, Billy," he said as he left the pilot house.

Captain Billy's jolly smile was quick, but his eyes, troubled, almost sad, didn't echo the smile.

Fargo moved down the steep outside stairway toward the bottom deck. As he reached the main, center deck, he almost collided with Darlene Binder. In a short black dress and bare shoulders, a white apron over the front of the dress, she held a cocktail tray in one hand.

"Just finished a break," she said, her wide mouth offering a quick, warm smile. Nice shoulders, Fargo noted, square and broad, her balanced breasts firmly held in by the wired top of the waitress outfit. "Coming into the salon?" she asked.

"Not likely." He smiled.

"I get off at midnight," she said, her eyes twinkling with appreciative appraisal as she took in the strong, chiseled cut of his face.

"I'll remember that."

"You going to be sailing with us for a while?"

"Depends." Fargo shrugged. "You always so full of questions?"

"I'm full of everything: warmth, curiosity, fun . . ."

"I'll remember that, too," Fargo said, and watched her hurry away, short skirt wriggling over a firm rear. Darlene Binder could be no more than she seemed, one of those curious, frank women who loved gossip and questions, social and sexual give-and-take. Or she could be more. He'd file Darlene in a corner of his mind for now.

Fargo continued on down to the main deck and leaned against the side of the boat. His gaze scanned the dark trees on both sides of the river. He watched the night grow deeper until most of the passenger cabins were darkened and only the gaming salon remained brightly lit. He strolled along the deck to pass the crew quarters, found it quiet and dark, and went on to the stable a few feet forward of the boiler room.

A kerosene lamp burned on low. He saw five stalls, all filled, the Ovaro in the first one. An emptied oats bucket hung on a wood peg and the horse whinnied in greeting as Fargo stepped to the stall and stroked the jet-black snout. He ran his hands over the horse's legs, up along the brisket and elbow on the forelegs, the stifle on the hind legs, feeling for swollen muscles and strained tendons. Satisfied there were none, he stroked the horse's neck for a few moments longer and then turned to leave with a quick glance at the other stalls.

Fargo suddenly froze in place, his brow creasing as he stared at the horse in the third stall. Even in the dim lamplight the horse's pale-bronze coat gleamed, his big form filling the stall. Fargo walked toward the horse and saw the full yellow-white mane on the powerful neck. "I'll be damned," he murmured aloud as he stopped before the horse. He knew only one palomino of such magnificence, and only one man who rode it. But he took another step closer to prove himself right. "Cormac," he said softly, and the horse's ears went up instantly. Fargo smiled and stepped back. "Canyon O'Grady, here on board. I'll be damned," he murmured again, and hurried from the stable with surprise still clinging to him. The world was full of coincidences, he told himself, yet with Canyon O'Grady coincidence was a word used with caution.

He paused, scanned the decks above. Canyon could be in one of the darkened cabins, but that wasn't likely, not for Canyon O'Grady with a gaming salon on hand. Fargo climbed to the middle deck of the riverboat where the light from the salon streamed into the night. He found a narrow door that opened onto an equally narrow balcony that looked down on the salon below. He halted and let his gaze take in the scene below. The room was well-filled with players, mostly men, but a generous sprinkling of women. The dice tables were against the far wall, surrounded by mostly men. The blackjack table was next. His eyes moved on to where a roulette table occupied the center of the room. He slowly moved along the balcony as it turned to border the other side of the salon and he halted again as he spied Monica Milford at the faro table almost directly below him.

Clad in a black gown as onyx as her hair, sleeveless and cut very low in front, with a deep V that showed the long curve of her breasts, she was strikingly beautiful. She played her game with cool, crisp efficiency while she radiated sensuousness, an exciting combination of fire and ice. It was small wonder few of her players won against her. Fargo smiled. They were probably unable to concentrate on their game. He let his gaze move on to where three poker tables occupied the opposite side of the room. One table, five players seated around it, held his gaze as he stared at one of the players. The tousled head of flaming red hair and devil-may-care roguish handsomeness marked only one man, Canyon O'Grady.

But Fargo's frown deepened as he moved around the narrow balcony until he was closer to the players below. Canyon O'Grady was decked out in a gray frock coat, he saw, replete with ruffled shirt, a pearl-gray cravat, and a diamond stickpin, the outfit of a riverboat gambler with just the proper touch of the dandy to it. Fargo smiled at the sight and the thought. Canyon O'Grady a riverboat gambler, he repeated. It was a role, of course, a masquerade, the trappings of deceit. But a role where he could use all the roguish smile and easy manner that was a natural part of him—indeed, a role almost tailored to the man. But it was, Fargo knew, no more than that, which meant that Canyon O'Grady was aboard the riverboat for his own very good reasons.

Fargo almost laughed aloud as he saw the stack of chips in front of Canyon and watched him pull in still another pile of winnings. He was playing his role well, making money at it. Fargo's eyes went to one of the other players, a short-necked figure in a black shirt. He saw the man slam his cards down as Canyon's flame-haired figure bent over the table to pull in a few strayed chips.

"Goddamn, nobody can be that lucky, mister," the man spit out.

"Not luck at all, my friend," Canyon said, and smiled. "It's called knowing how to play one's cards."

"You've been cheating all along," the black-shirted man shouted as he jumped to his feet. A silence fell over the salon at once, and Fargo saw Canyon O'Grady's face remain expressionless.

"I'm going to make believe I didn't hear that," Canyon said quietly as he counted chips.

"You heard it, you goddamn four-flusher," the man threw back. He wasn't about to be placated. He wanted to take his losings back by gun, Fargo saw, and out of the corner of his eye he saw the two figures move behind Canyon. The black-shirted man was stacking the odds for his own final deal.

"He doesn't cheat," Monica Milford's voice cut in. "He's been playing here for a month. I'd know if he cheated."

"Butt out, bitch," the black-shirted man said, and Fargo unholstered the big Colt at his side. The man took a step back, and Fargo saw that Canyon had stopped counting chips, his snapping blue eyes on the man in front of him. Other than that he hadn't moved. The man took another step backward to give himself more room to draw, his right arm dangling loosely at his side. But Fargo's eyes were on the two gunslingers behind Canyon. They were the real danger. The black-shirted man was about to commit suicide though he didn't know it.

Fargo raised the Colt in his hand, his eyes narrowed. It would take perfect timing. He'd have to fire the moment Canyon did, while the two in back were still drawing. It would hinge on split seconds, but that was nothing new to him. Winning was often a matter of split seconds. The man on the left first, he decided, and he flicked a glance at Canyon O'Grady, saw the snapping blue eyes were no longer roguishly smiling.

"You lost your money. Don't add your life," the flame-haired man said.

"I'm taking my money back now," the black-shirted man growled, stupid, braggart's words that telegraphed his move.

Fargo saw him reach for his gun and glimpsed the flash of movement that was Canyon's arm. Fargo's finger tightened on the trigger of the Colt and one of the two men behind Canyon flew back in his own fountain of red. Fargo heard Canyon's shot explode, but his own Colt had shifted, fired again. The second man, his gun only half out of its holster, doubled almost in two as he pitched to the floor.

Fargo's eyes glanced back to Canyon standing beside the table and saw the black-shirted man spread-eagle, facedown on the floor, his shirt as much red as black now.

Canyon, coolly holstering his big Colt with the ivory grips, lifted his head to peer up at the narrow balcony. Fargo wasn't sure if he'd seen a fleeting smile touch the roguish face, but he nodded as Canyon executed a bow of appreciation. Fargo walked to the stairs at the end of the balcony and went down to the floor of the salon.

Monica hurried toward him, her hand on Canyon's arm, as, behind her, crewmen were pulling away the three inert forms.

"This is Skye Fargo, Canyon," she introduced. "He's a special friend of Caroline's."

"Now he's a special friend of mine," Canyon said smoothly, and extended his hand. "Canyon O'Grady it is."

"My pleasure," Fargo said, taking the outstretched hand.

"I'm indebted. I never saw those two backshooters," the flame-haired man said.

"I happened to be at the right place at the right time," Fargo said. "It's happened to me."

"Has it, now?" Canyon smiled. "It still calls for a drink. I'm in Cabin Twelve. Meet you there in a few minutes."

"Sounds good," Fargo said with a pleasant smile. He turned away as Canyon accompanied Monica to the faro table and the rest of the salon began to settle down. He smiled as he remembered Captain Billy's remark about Monica having become "real friendly with a gambling man." It was even more understandable now that he knew who the gambling man was.

Fargo had reached the outside deck when he saw Caroline hurrying toward him, the very round breasts bouncing as her heels came down hard on the deck.

"I'd just finished dressing when I heard the shots. I got to the salon just after it ended," she said. "Mr. O'Grady was very lucky you were there."

"A gambling man's supposed to have luck," Fargo said.

"I told Captain Billy about it just now. He couldn't leave the wheel, what with Ez not on board. He told me to thank you for helping."

"I'm here to help. It was a side trail," Fargo said with a shrug.

Her round brown eyes appraised him for a long

moment. "You'll be staying on watch through the rest of the night, I take it."

"You take it right."

"Take my cabin again, come morning," she offered.

"Of course, you'll be up and out."

"Of course."

"I'll do that," he said. "If I don't get a better offer."

Her eyes grew instantly disapproving and she brushed past him without another word.

He strolled on, went inside the boat again to find Cabin Twelve. Halfway down a corridor, he found Darlene Binder at the doorway of a cabin. She was still in her short-skirted waitress outfit with the little white apron. She had the legs of a sixteen-year-old, he noted, smooth and shapely.

"I was in a corner of the salon. That was really something," she said admiringly.

"Unexpected interruption." Fargo shrugged.

"You're really something," Darlene said, frank interest in her eyes. "I like men who are something special. How about a nightcap?"

"Sorry. O'Grady offered me one. I'm on my way there now," Fargo told her.

"And well he should," Darlene said.

"Some other time," Fargo said. "But not tonight."

"Staying on watch?"

"You have it."

Her wide mouth offered a tantalizing smile. "You can stop in when you're finished. I'll leave the door latch open."

"I'll be wanting sleep then."

"I'll be sleeping late. I don't start work till supper," Darlene said. "We could wake up together."

"And then?" He grinned.

"Whatever," she returned.

"I'll keep it in mind," Fargo said, and moved on as Darlene entered her room. Cabin Two-A, he noted. The offer would indeed stay in his mind, though not for the reasons she'd think. Darlene seemed a garrulous type. She might well be the quick way to finding out more about the regulars on the *Shady Lady*. Knowledge gained through pleasure was the best kind . . . He smiled.

4

Canyon O'Grady closed the cabin door and shed his gray frock jacket. The fancy cravat and diamond stickpin came next and then he unbuttoned the ruffled shirt. God, he hated the precious outfit, he muttered inwardly. He lay back across the bed at an angle and ran one hand through his flame-red hair. He'd been careless tonight. He should've expected the man might have had partners. He'd be dead now if it hadn't been for Fargo, he realized. He'd let himself grow increasingly frustrated with the role. It had been over a month and he'd come up with nothing.

Except for Monica. She'd been the only good thing so far, and his face found its usual rakish smile. Until tonight, he snorted. Skye Fargo here, aboard the boat, the one man he could trust implicitly and perhaps the one man who could help. A stroke of luck if ever there was one, Canyon reflected. Monica had told him the captain's niece was trying to bring someone aboard to put a stop to the strange, nighttime raids on the boat, but Canyon never dreamed it'd be Fargo. O'Grady smiled again as old memories flooded over him, those times he and Fargo had worked together, fought side by side, pooled skills and insights. They'd been successful, each of them. Maybe this could be another time.

All he knew was that up to now he had watched, listened, waited, played his role, which gave him the freedom to move about easily, and he'd uncovered nothing. Yet his inner senses tingled. Something was going on, under his very nose, yet he'd come onto nothing. Fargo would be full of questions. He'd want to know all of it, and that's what he'd get: everything just as it had been given him. Canyon let his mind reel backwards—the time, just before midnight; the place, Washington, capital of the nation.

The large room had glowed in a soft light, the old, European-designed furniture all replaced by pieces made by American furniture-makers. The man who had ordered the change sat in the Thomas Sheraton high-backed leather chair, his eyes a bright, snapping blue, the unruly tuft of white hair rising from just above his forehead, the very personal mark of President James Buchanan. His eyes smiled as he surveyed the flame-haired man seated across from him.

"We haven't many of you, Canyon O'Grady," President Buchanan said. "Maybe six government agents altogether, and you're the best of the best. That's why I'm tossing this kettle of fish in your lap. And a kettle of fish it is, indeed."

"At your service, Mr. President." Canyon smiled.

"That, and one more reason," the president said, and his eyes took on a twinkle. "I know that a son of old Ireland will take special pleasure in tweaking the tail of the British lion."

"Spoken as a son of Irish parents or as President of the United States?"

"A little of both." James Buchanan laughed.

"Now, how do I go about this tail-tweaking, Mr. President?"

James Buchanan's face grew sober at once. "It won't be easy, I'll tell you that. There are a lot of players in this kettle. Maybe we can only get a few of them." The president rose, paced up and down the room for a moment before halting in front of Canyon. "There are dark clouds hanging over the nation. You know that, O'Grady."

"Clouds of secession," Canyon murmured, and the president nodded gravely.

"Some hope the next president, probably Mr. Lincoln, can chase them away. Few of us have much confidence in that, and in the southern states, they're preparing. The South has chosen a president, Jefferson Davis, and military commanders, Pierre Beauregard, Joseph Johnston, and Robert E. Lee. This has gone far beyond talk now," the president said.

"I expect the government has its own plans," Canyon said, the shadow of a question in his voice.

"Yes, but up to now it's all been pretty much in the nature of countermoves," Buchanan said. "The southern states have been very busy trying to prepare themselves in every area. One of the most important is money. A secession is going to need money, a lot of money."

"How does the British lion come into this?"

"The South has asked the English for large amounts of money."

"How do they expect to get it?"

"They know that most of the English clothing industry depends on cotton from the southern states. It'd take the English trading companies a long time over great distances to replace their imports of American cotton. So, to guarantee the continued shipment of cotton, they've asked the English for large sums in advance."

"Wheels inside wheels," Canyon muttered.

"But the English do not want a face-off with the American government. They don't want to be seen as financing a possible secession, so they officially refused the request from the southern states," President Buchanan said. "Lord Upshaw, the British minister of trade, assured me himself that her majesty's government will stay uninvolved."

Canyon's lips pursed as he regarded the president. "You sound unconvinced," he murmured.

Buchanan smiled. "Uninvolved. An interesting word, that. It can be translated into looking the other way."

"You think that's what they're doing?"

"We're certain of it. They look the other way while the private industry groups, like the Import Shippers' Association, carry the ball. The South tripled cotton shipments during the past three months. Our intelligence tells us the English groups are smuggling gold to the South by way of Mississippi riverboats."

"Mississippi riverboats?" Canyon echoed with a frown. "Why such a roundabout way when they can bring it in by ship to any of the Gulf ports?"

"Because American frigates are stopping and searching every British merchantman the moment it enters American waters," President Buchanan said with a note of satisfaction. "We caught one gold shipment months ago, and they've stopped now. We're convinced they're bringing the gold in from Canada—disguised, of course—then using the riverboats to sail downriver with it to the southern-state ports, maybe Memphis but probably St. Louis."

"I'm to get aboard a riverboat, find out how they're bringing it in, and put a stop to it," Canyon said, and the president nodded.

"One riverboat in particular, the *Shady Lady*. Intelligence tells us that's probably the boat they're using."

"Why?"

"The others sail from the Gulf ports, New Orleans to Memphis and back again. The *Shady Lady*'s the only one that sails from St. Louis north into Minnesota Territory ports. That's where the gold has to be brought aboard, so that's our riverboat," Buchanan said. "The gold is vital to them. You can be sure they've made extensive plans to ensure getting it. We don't know what they all are, but we're certain they've an agent on board."

"You know anything more than that?"

"No. It could be one of the passengers or a member of the ship's personnel. You might be able to find out, or you might not. Meanwhile, you'll have to be damn careful," the president said.

"I will, sir." Canyon nodded.

The president stood and extended his hand. "It's in your hands, Agent O'Grady. Remember, your government doesn't want the British lion financing a secession through a side door."

"Mr. President, let's hope the next sound you hear will be that of a lion getting his tail tweaked."

The fine room swam away, the white-haired man dissolved, and Canyon heard the knock on the door. He rose, pulled it open, and Fargo stepped into the cabin. No proper smiles this time, no distant politeness, not on either man's part as the room exploded in exuberant greetings and laughter.

"I couldn't believe my eyes when I saw Cormac in the stable," Fargo said.

"And I'd trouble believing mine when I saw you on the balcony, lad," Canyon O'Grady returned.

"Fill me in," Fargo said. "What changed Canyon O'Grady the tinker into Canyon O'Grady the fancy gambling man? What are you up to?"

"Being frustrated so far," Canyon growled, and began to tell Fargo all the details of his assignment. The Trailsman listened in silence till he finished, and then he let a soft sigh of air rush from his lips in a low whistle.

"This does have all kinds of players," Fargo murmured. "English cotton importers, southern agents, and her majesty's government in the wings. Plus hired help, I'd guess."

"I'm sure of that." Canyon grimaced.

"You checked out the cargo taken aboard?" Fargo questioned.

"Anything that could resemble gold bars. I spot-checked boxes, barrels, crates, personal trunks. I can't do a thorough check without blowing my cover. I have to sneak around, grab a quick opportunity, and leave. I think if I could pinpoint their agent on board, I'd be able to get somewhere. But it could be damn near anybody, including one of the passengers. Some make regular trips on the boat."

"You'll find a lead," Fargo said.

"I heard about Captain Billy's niece calling in someone over the Indian raids. I sure as hell never thought it'd be you, Fargo."

"Old friends, new favors." Fargo shrugged. "What can you tell me about the raids?"

"Not a hell of a lot, lad. I knew they were happening, but I didn't rush out to get into it. I have to protect my image. I'm a riverboat gambling man, not a gunfighter ready to step into a fight at the drop of a hat."

"Seems nobody did much. Ez Crawley, the first mate, had his own reasons for staying safe."

"You don't believe them."

"I'm not sure. I am convinced somebody on board is tied into it. It has to be. Somebody got word to the dry-gulchers that damn near killed me," Fargo said.

"Three crewmen were killed in the raids. That puts a lid on heroes," Canyon suggested.

"I suppose so. You see, I think the raids are an excuse, a mask. Indians don't go around stealing sacks of grain. I don't even think they're Indians."

Canyon felt his brows furrow. "That's real interesting."

"Caroline told me that the captain is on the hook for the value of the shipments stolen. That's a lot of money, more than he has. The only way he could pay is to put the boat up for sale."

"And somebody else will take over the boat and the route," Canyon said.

"Bull's-eye. Somebody who's dealing the cards, so it's bound to happen," Fargo said.

"Any ideas who?"

"No, and I don't care who at the moment. I want the raids stopped first. Then we can close down on who."

Canyon put his head back and a laugh escaped his lips. "Now, isn't this a fine coming together, old friend? We've been brought to the same place by two sets of rascals, gold smugglers and southern agents for me, fake river raiders for you. I'm thinking you'll catch yours before I catch mine."

Fargo's eyes narrowed at Canyon. "You're not one for casual observations. Meaning what, exactly?"

"You'll have all that time left to help me," Canyon said, his snapping blue eyes twinkling.

"Agreed." Fargo laughed. "If you keep your eyes and ears open for anything, that'll help me."

"You know I will, lad. It'll be good working together again."

"We did pretty damn well the last times," Fargo said.

"That we did," Canyon said.

"Maybe the lovely Monica can help you hear things. I hear you're very friendly."

"Tongues do wag." Canyon smiled. "She's the best thing that's happened to me on this damn boat until you showed up. She's beautiful, warm, and intelligent. It's not easy to find a woman where you can enjoy both her mind and her body. She'll be coming by any minute now."

"My cue to leave," Fargo said. "Draw her out. See if she knows anything that could help me."

"I'll do that," Canyon said.

"You going to tell her we didn't just meet?"

"Hell, no, lad. Not for now, anyway. You know I play it close to the vest." Canyon walked to the cabin door with Fargo. "I owe you one for tonight, lad."

"Nobody's keeping score," Fargo answered.

"That's true enough." Canyon laughed and watched the big man with the lake-blue eyes and black hair stride down the corridor. The agent turned back into the cabin, took off the ruffled shirt, and lay down across the bed again. He felt better than he had since arriving aboard the *Shady Lady*. Fargo was a welcome sight in any case. It would be good to be able to share thoughts with someone.

O'Grady felt a small sigh escape his lips. He loved the life he had chosen. Being a United States government agent gave him the freedom to be largely his own boss and challenged both mental and physical skills. It let him range far and wide across the untamed country, wearing whatever hat seemed appropriate. But he missed the sharing of thoughts, problems, feelings. Sharing was one of life's most rewarding things. Perhaps especially the sharing of problems, he smiled wryly. To have to keep everything in constantly, to always keep one's own counsel, was to live with aloneness. Not loneliness. Aloneness. There was a difference.

Every once in a while it reached him, as it had this night, flaring up to make him miss the sharing more than usual. But, then, aloneness was in his blood. He had been born to it. It had been his father's lot and that of his father's father, the lot of all who fought for liberty and freedom from the time of Wolfe Tone and the croppies, the Young Ireland Movement and James Connolly and Padraic Pearse and Fintan Lalor. They had all known aloneness, the soul-searing apartness of being strangers in their own land, hunted sons in their beloved country. Those who stayed to hide and those who fled to fight again, such as his own father . . . they all held the knowing inside them.

And now he, in a different way, in a different land, he carried on the spirit that rose up against injustice, wrong and the ruthless and callous crimes committed by the powerful on the weak. Outlaws and despots were not always governments. But this time there was a difference. This time there were echoes of other injustices in other places. Yet he had found nothing concrete, and frustration had become a hairshirt, irritating, clinging, mocking. He had watched the unloadings at St. Louis and found only ordinary freight outfits picking up ordinary merchandise, much of which he had checked out on board himself.

He found himself concentrating on figures standing by: the intentness of their faces, a tense body movement, an attitude, anything that would set them apart. Wagon drivers could be hired—haulage outfits also, he realized. But it was unlikely such vital shipments would be left to an ordinary haulage crew. There'd be somebody watching to make certain everything went off according to plan. Yet he had found nothing and seen no one that fit the picture. The *Shady Lady* had made six round trips to St. Louis since he'd come aboard. Only at the very first had he seen a figure, standing apart and watching the ship unload. But the man had vanished into the dockside crowds before he could be reached and there'd been no once since. Canyon found himself wondering if perhaps there'd been a massive mistake in intelligence information. Maybe there were no gold shipments being sent by riverboat.

The knock at the door exploded away his musings. He rose, pulled the door open, and a tall, willowy figure stepped into the cabin. Monica Milford paused, reached up, and brushed his lips with a quick kiss. "Saw your new friend, Fargo, going out onto the lower deck," she said. "I guessed he'd just left you."

"You guessed right."

Monica walked to the bed and lowered herself down at the edge of it. "He has quite a reputation, according to Caroline. Deservedly, from what I saw tonight," she said.

"Yes, I've heard about him myself."

Monica stretched long, lovely legs out and leaned

back on the bed on her elbows. "He expects to help Captain Billy with the raids. He tell you how?"

"Stop them first, then find out who's behind them."

"I was told they were Indian raids." Monica frowned.

"He thinks there's more than meets the eye," Canyon told her.

"Such as?"

"He's not sure about that himself, yet."

She shrugged. "Seemed like plain old Indians to me."

Canyon stepped in front of her, put both hands on her shoulders. "You come here to talk about Fargo?"

"No, I was just curious," Monica said, a slow smile coming to her lips. "I came to look after my favorite gambling man."

"That's better," Canyon said as his hands slowly slid the thin spaghetti straps of her black gown over her shoulders. He touched a clasp at the back, and the bodice opened and slid to her waist. He took in the beautifully curved breasts, pale-white skin making the pink tips appear rosier than they were against the faint pink circles. He cupped both breasts in his hands, squeezed gently, and let his thumbs move over the soft rosy nipples.

Monica gave a tiny shudder and rose; the black dress fell to the floor. She pushed undergarments after it and stood beautifully naked in front of him. Her long legs held together, a curly triangle an onyx patch against her skin, abdomen flat, hips curving up into a narrow waist.

"O woman! lovely woman! Nature made thee/To temper man: we had been brutes without you," Canyon murmured.

"And who do you quote now, gambling man?"

"Thomas Otway, a seventeenth-century poet," Canyon said. "And man of rare perception."

Monica stepped to him, helped him undo his belt and pull off clothes. When his own nakedness touched hers, he felt the soft, tantalizing pressure of her nipples against his broad chest. Monica's hands began to move slowly down his body until, reaching low, she found his already burgeoning warmth. He heard the tiny shudder escape her. He wrapped arms around her, and half-lifted her from the floor with a sudden, almost rough movement. He fell onto the bed with her still enclosed in his arms. It had been that way the first time and they'd made a small ritual of it, just as the courting dance of the sage grouse is both a stimulus and a herald.

Monica's lips found his, warm, pressing, opening for him. Her hand fluttered up and down his body, caressing, smoothing, suddenly coming to a halt to curl around him. Again the shudder of delight went through her.

Canyon allowed himself time to enjoy the beauty of her breasts, a trifle long, yet full and curving into deep cups where the tiny nipples were but pink dots. He brought his face down to one pale-white mound, pulled the tiny pink tip with his lips, and sucked gently on it, drew it in, caressed it with slow, circular motions of his tongue.

Monica's gasp echoed in the cabin and her hand found him again, quickly this time, hurrying strokes, and he heard soft cries well from her throat.

"Please, please," she murmured. "Don't make me wait. Oh, God, no, no." Monica's hips twisted, slid under him, and her hands clasped around him. She pulled him to her with a cry of frantic urgency. "Please,

please . . . oh, oh . . . aaaaaah," she groaned as his pulsating warmth found her, slid smoothly forward, filling the sweet sheath.

Monica half-screamed, her fingernails digging into his back. She lifted her torso, her onyx triangle brushing against him, and her pale-white skin seemed to grow even whiter. Tiny blue veins throbbed in her neck as she pushed and thrust with him. Sensations engulfed him, wondrous, satisfying sensations, but it was almost as pleasurable to watch Monica's face mirror her ecstasy as her soft moaning sounds surged to curl into the air. Her body lifted, twisted, the full-cupped breasts swaying as every inch of her being enjoyed the pleasures of the senses.

As always, O'Grady found himself being swept along faster and faster by her cries, her frantic surges and the small screams of demand, but he managed to hold back until he saw her slender body begin to quiver. The tiny pink nipples first, then the lovely breasts trembling, and finally all of her quivering and her long legs squeezing hard against his ribs.

"Now, now. Oh, God, now . . . iiiieeee, oh, oh," Monica screamed against his chest, and he exploded with her, the volcano of pleasure that was forever too much and not enough. He heard his own groan as his face fell forward to press against the pale-white mounds.

When Monica finally fell back and drew in deep gasps of breath, he stayed with her, his head pressed into the downy cushions, her warmth still encompassing him. "More wonderful each time," Monica murmured, arms holding his face to her.

"Because you're more wonderful each time, lass," Canyon breathed, and meant each word. Finally he slid from her and she gave a tiny groan but half-turned on one side and rose onto one elbow, her hair falling loosely to make a dark halo. She ran one finger idly across his smooth chest.

"How did you ever become a gambling man, Canyon O'Grady?" she asked. "You're different than any I've ever known."

"Different?" He frowned.

"The others all had a touch of the snake-in-the-grass about them. You've none of that," she said. "And all I've known carried a derringer or a pocket pistol, and you carry a big Colt with ivory grips. And I've never known one who could quote the poets as you do." He laughed softly and she rose up straighter, one breast resting against his chest with soft warmth. "You're really something of a mystery, Canyon O'Grady. What were you before you became a gambling man?"

"I've told you that, lass—a wanderer, a tinker, a minstrel."

"Singing only love songs, I'll wager," Monica said, and ran one hand through the flame-red hair.

"Now, that'd be telling." Canyon laughed. "And what have you to say about a beautiful young lass that's a faro dealer? That's twice the mystery, I'm thinking."

"No mystery if you had a father that was a faro dealer," Monica returned. "He made believe I was the son he always wanted and never had. He taught me to be a faro dealer, to ride like a man, and to drink like a lady."

"It seems neither of us fits the usual mold. Maybe that's why it happened so fast between us." It had been fast, an instant attraction at their first meeting that flared almost immediately into more than words.

"Maybe," Monica agreed. "I've no better answer. It happened faster than ever before for me."

"All that loveliness of yours had something to do with it on my side."

"And all that roguish charm and flame-topped handsomeness of yours on my side," Monica murmured. She shifted position and curled herself tight against him and was fast asleep in minutes.

He let himself enjoy the beauty of her smoothness, the way her hip rose in a high curve to taper down to the long leg. When he reached over to turn out the lamp, a wry smile edged his lips. Things always seemed better with Monica's lovely nakedness against him. He'd once tried questioning her about the crew and passengers and pulled back immediately. She had been entirely too quick, he'd realized, too sharp to be manipulated, and she had questioned him in return. One of these days he'd take her into his confidence, Canyon mused. But not yet . . .

He closed his eyes and slept against her warm softness.

5

Fargo stretched his long, muscled body against the wood stacked at the side of the boiler-room wall. He had spent the major part of the night scanning the inky blackness of the shore and had seen nothing. Now the remaining minutes of the night swept away with equal quiet as the first faint pink streaks of the new day slid across the sky.

Fargo rose, stretched again, and moved down the low deck. He found a door to the inside corridor and finally halted before Cabin Two-A. He closed one big hand around the doorknob and carefully turned the brass knob. The door came open and he smiled. Darlene was a woman of her word. He stepped silently into the room. The gray dawn was filtering through a lone, curtained window, and he found the figure atop the bed, clad in a blue nightgown.

Darlene Binder slept with legs and arms stretched out in all directions, he noted. She stayed fast asleep and he turned away, quietly shed clothes down to his underdrawers, and stretched out on the braided rug on the cabin floor. He let himself quickly fall asleep and he stayed asleep until the sudden motion of the boat woke him, a soft bump and then a dull scrape. The *Shady Lady* was docking at Moline.

Fargo pushed up on one elbow to see that Darlene hadn't even blinked in her sleep. But she had changed position, one leg thrown out at an angle as she lay on her side and one breast curved up over the edge of the neck of the nightgown. He lay back on the rug again and listened to the dim sounds of loading and finally felt the riverboat slowly move on once more. He closed his eyes and welcomed the additional hours of sleep.

When he came awake again, it was the sound of Darlene stirring and sitting up. He saw her swing both legs over the edge of the bed and surprise flood her face as she saw him. "I'll be damned," Darlene breathed.

"Surprise," Fargo said.

"I never heard you come in." Darlene frowned.

"That was the idea." Fargo smiled and pushed to a sitting position.

Darlene sat at the edge of the bed and vigorously shook her head, her curly brown hair flying from side to side. Her breasts shook along, he noted, until she stopped and pushed to her feet. She started for a narrow, tall screen in a corner of the cabin and he glimpsed the edge of a washbasin behind it.

"There's a bathroom outside to the left you can use," Darlene said as she disappeared behind the screen. He rose, pulled on trousers, and went outside into the corridor. He found the bathroom and washed and freshened up. When he returned to the cabin, Darlene was still in her nightgown. With her hair brushed, her face washed, and without powder or paint, the years showed more in the little crinkles around her eyes and the tightening lines under her chin. But with her good facial planes and wide, attractive mouth, Darlene Binder was still a most appealing woman, part of the appeal made up of her frank, open sensuality.

"I come back too soon?" Fargo asked, his lake-blue eyes moving across the nightgown.

"No, I like to lounge around before I dress for work," Darlene said. "Come and sit down." She slid across the bedsheet on her rump to make room for him, and her eyes lingered on the powerfully muscled chest as he lowered himself to the edge of the bed.

"We stopped at Moline. Guess Ez Crawley is back on board now," Fargo said idly.

"I'm sure of it."

"He make many shore trips during an average run?"

"Yes. Ez is the kind of riverboat man who needs shore leave. Sometimes he just goes to a saloon and gets himself drunk," Darlene said.

"Or finds a girl?"

Darlene's lips pursed as she thought for a moment. "Maybe, but I don't think Ez is much of a ladies' man. He's too much the loner to let anyone get close to him."

"Anybody else in the crew go ashore regularly?" Fargo pressed.

"They all do when they get the chance, mostly at overnight stops."

Fargo nodded and grimaced inwardly at the reply. "Any of the regular passengers get on and off a lot?"

"Not really. They mostly stay on till they reach where they're going."

"But there are regular passengers," Fargo said.

"Sure, some businessmen, some drummers, a few family men who go back and forth," Darlene said. She paused and gave him a slightly wry smile. "Now who's full of questions?"

"Sorry." Fargo shrugged. "Thanks for the use of the room."

"You could've come into bed."

"Didn't think that would be proper," Fargo said, and Darlene's lips pursed again as she fastened him with an appraising stare.

"You know, Fargo, I'd guess a lot of things could bother you, but being proper would be at the bottom of the list," she commented. His laugh was an admission and she sniffed in satisfaction. "You came just to ask questions," she said.

"For now," Fargo said.

"That's called being polite."

"It's called being honest," Fargo said. "You're a very attractive woman. I just want to move slowly."

She leaned forward and her lips found his—warm, full, her wide mouth enveloping—and she smiled as she pulled back. "That's to help you move less slowly."

"I imagine it'll do that." Fargo nodded and began to pull on clothes as Darlene watched. She went to the cabin door with him when he was ready to leave. She kissed him again, and was still smiling when he stepped outside and out onto the open deck.

The late-afternoon shadows were already gathering, he noted. He climbed to the pilot house, where he found Ez Crawley's tall, lank form at the wheel. The man's dour, deeply creased face turned to him as he came in.

"Captain Billy's sleeping. He'll be at the wheel tonight," the man said.

"Thanks," Fargo said. "You have a good time ashore?"

"Nothing special," Ez Crawley said as he peered forward across the boat's prow.

"You visit friends?" Fargo asked idly.

"No friends. I like being alone."

"Some people do," Fargo said pleasantly as he strolled out of the pilot house. He went down the outside companionway and had reached the deck when he saw Caroline striding toward him. Her very round, high breasts bounced under a pink blouse tucked into a dark blue skirt. Even her glower didn't destroy her round-cheeked prettiness, but he saw the anger in her eyes as she halted before him.

"You never came to the cabin," she snapped. "I presume you got that better offer?"

"Maybe," Fargo said blandly.

"How could you?"

"How could I what?"

"It was Darlene, wasn't it?"

"What makes you say that?"

"I saw her talking to you late last night," Caroline snapped. "And I remember the girl in the cabin. You don't miss an opportunity."

"You jump to conclusions. I wanted to see what I could learn from her."

"Did you learn anything?" Caroline snapped.

"She answered my questions. I wanted to find out who on board went ashore often. She told me."

Caroline's eyes narrowed at him. "Except about herself, I'll bet."

"Meaning what?"

"She goes ashore with anyone she can. Darling Darlene she's called, the sweetheart of every traveling drummer that comes aboard," Caroline flung at him. "So you didn't dip into anything exclusive."

"My, you have developed a way with words, haven't you, honey?"

"Maybe you just bring it out in a person." Caroline glared, almost stamped her foot, and looked out into the river.

"Not that it's any of your damn business, but I didn't dip into anything, exclusive or not," he said as she continued to glare across the water, her round cheeks flushed. He reached a hand out, took her by one shoulder, and turned her to him. "You brought me here to help Captain Billy. I'll do it my way. Don't interfere."

Caroline's lips thinned and relaxed after a moment. "All right, I won't. I didn't mean to interfere. I apologize for that. But I've a right to my own thoughts," she said stubbornly.

"You do," Fargo said. "Try being grownup while you're having them." He turned and strode away.

"Thank you for the advice," she called after him, each word sheathed in ice. She didn't see his smile as he rounded the corner of the deck and saw the tall, flame-haired figure leaning against one of the stanchions.

"Little Miss Caroline is disenchanted with her savior," Canyon said wryly.

"Miss Caroline's unhappy with everything. Coming to me was an act of desperation. She may be unhappy, angry, scared, disappointed, but I'll bet she's the only one on board who really cares what happens to Captain Billy."

"The others couldn't be expected to care the way she does. They're not kin," Canyon observed.

"Kin often doesn't give a damn," Fargo pointed out.

"True enough."

"She's the kind who can really care."

Canyon's eyes moved slowly across the Mississippi.

"That's important. Real caring is important in a woman. When a woman cares, it's the one time she stops calculating."

Fargo felt his brows rise. "That's a surprising remark from you, Canyon O'Grady, last of the great romantics. Are you telling me that's all a mask?"

"No, I'm a romantic, but even a romantic can be permitted bouts of cynicism. Alexander Pope was certainly a romantic, yet he wrote that every woman is a rake at heart," Canyon said. "Apologies, old friend, I'm feeling frustrated. I've been here a month without picking up one lead, not on the gold bars and not on any southern agent. If he's aboard, he hasn't made any mistakes."

"You haven't any leads, and I've too many," Fargo snorted. "A hell of a lot of people leave the boat damn often. Any of them could've carried the message about my coming to help or even set up raids."

"Work on it, lad. Get it over with so you can give me a hand. I sure seem to need one," Canyon said.

"I'll be trying. Meanwhile, you've Monica to help make you feel better."

"Thank God for Monica," Canyon said. "You know where I'll be later." He hurried away.

Fargo strolled to the dining room on the second deck, an oblong room painted white and gold. Darlene appeared in her working outfit of short black dress and white apron. He ordered a steak sandwich and a bourbon.

"Going to come visiting again this morning?" Darlene smiled.

"Can't say," he returned, and Caroline's words tumbled through his mind. He decided against any further exploring for now. Maybe Darlene had simply excluded herself because he hadn't asked specifically. Or maybe she'd mentioned nothing about her own frequent trips to shore for very definite reasons. He'd wait and watch, Darlene now as much a question mark as a source of information.

He had finished the meal when she returned to the table, her wide smile frankly inviting. "You don't have to stay on deck and watch all night. Come to the cabin earlier. If anything happens outside, you'll hear it," Darlene said. "And wake me up this time."

"Maybe," he allowed with a smile, and she moved away with a wriggle of her very compact rear. He rose and went outside to find that night had descended, an almost moonless night with a clouded sky.

The riverboat made its own circle of light as it sailed downriver, almost as though it were a floating island removed from the rest of the world.

Fargo climbed to the pilot house, where Captain Billy was at the wheel. The captain turned as Fargo entered, tossed a wide smile back while keeping both hands on the big ship's wheel. "Thought I'd watch from up here for a while," Fargo said.

"Glad to have you," Captain Billy said. "Caroline sometimes keeps me company, but she's working on the ledger in her cabin tonight."

Fargo found a tall stool in a corner of the pilot house and perched atop it so he could peer out of the forward window. He frowned as he tried to separate the blackness of the moonless night. "Damned if I can see much," he remarked.

"It takes getting used to," Billy said, his round face wrinkling in a chuckle. "But it is hard on nights like this. You pick a spot a dozen yards in front of the bow and focus on it. There's always a little light from the sparks in the smokestack."

Fargo followed the instructions and the dark ribbon of the river just in front of the boat began to take on a murky definition. "Ez Crawley been with you long?" he asked casually.

"About ten years," Captain Billy said. "You're not thinking Ez is involved in this thing, are you?"

"I'm not thinking anybody is," Fargo said. "Or isn't."

"I appreciate your coming to help, Fargo, but anytime you want to pack it in, you just do so. I'll understand. A man can only waste so much of his time. I told Caroline that. This is our problem."

"She cares about you."

"She's a fine girl, but sometimes things just go bad and there's nothing anyone can do about it," Billy said, and Fargo again noticed the discouragement in the man. The years seemed to have worn him down indeed.

The Trailsman fell silent and strained his eyes to peer into the darkness outside, the bow of the boat an almost ghostly white as it moved slowly through the water. A bend in the river appeared and he watched Captain Billy steer the *Shady Lady* through the curve with just enough headway to keep it from drifting. They had just finished rounding the bend when Fargo saw Captain Billy's hands flash as he pulled levers and shouted into the wide-mouthed opening of a tube to the boiler room. "Shut off power," Billy shouted, and Fargo half-rose from the stool to strain his eyes over the prow of the boat.

"Damn," the captain swore softly as the long, wavy object took shape, looking not unlike some ghostly apparition with a hundred probing tentacles. But the tentacles were interlocking tree branches that kept rising out of the river, dripping water from their twisted arms. They seemed to reach out to the riverboat as they spread and grew taller and wider.

"Damn sawyer," Captin Billy hissed. "We're lucky it didn't come up beneath us and foul the paddle wheel."

The huge tangled obstacle of gnarled branches and tree trunks moved rhythmically up and down in the water, as if it were some monstrous gorgon beckoning with its snakelike hair.

"How long will it stay there?" Fargo asked.

"You never know. Never saw one that came up for less than a half-hour," Billy said. "I have to stay at the wheel in case we start to drift."

Fargo peered out at the river obstacle, and the river man's name of "sawyer" didn't fit at all. It was far too mild for the ominous appearance of the object that swayed in front of them.

The great paddle wheel stilled, silence engulfed the riverboat as it sat in the water. Occasionally, a tinkle of glasses and a woman's high-pitched laugh drifted from the salon. But suddenly, Fargo's wild-creature hearing caught another sound. His brow furrowing, he listened harder and heard it again, the soft slap of water against wood. He half-spun as he snapped his eyes to the shore. The dark, slender shapes took form, moved out from both shores, and he cursed as he flung the pilot-house door open and ran outside onto the deck.

"Canoes," he bit out. They were moving swiftly through the water toward the *Shady Lady* from both sides. Not just canoes, he corrected himself as he made out a square log raft paddled by four figures. He ran down the companionway to the lowest deck, the

Colt in his hand. He had just started for the rail when the first hail of arrows filled the night. He dived onto his stomach as their feathered shafts slammed into the ship on both sides of him.

The first line of the canoes had already reached the ship. Half-naked forms vaulted onto the deck when the second volley erupted, gunfire this time. They had both bow and rifles, he grimaced as he rolled behind one of the deck posts, came up on one knee, and fired.

One of the figures toppled into the river, and his second shot sent another falling overboard. But, like a horde of ants, the half-naked figures swarmed onto the lower deck of the boat. Some dropped to send another volley of gunfire at him and he ducked behind the post as wood splinters flew from it. At least a half-dozen of the apparent Indians had already raced into the cargo room.

Fargo glimpsed the log raft moving against the other side of the riverboat. The volley of rifle fire had ended and he glanced up to see more dark, slender forms racing into the cargo room. He fired again and a third figure fell, this one onto the deck. A heavy rifle shot exploded and Fargo glanced up at the deck above to see Caroline, in a pale-yellow nightgown, fire another shot from a heavy old Hawkens plains rifle. He also saw four half-naked forms racing up to the deck and reach it before Caroline could reload.

"Damn," Fargo swore as he raced up to the deck just as two crewmen appeared, rifles in hand. They were both cut down by a hail of arrows from below. As he flew up the companionway steps, he heard the dull thump of the sacks of wheat and grain being tossed onto the log raft on the other side of the vessel.

He reached the deck just as two of the attackers seized Caroline, a third ducking the blow she aimed at him with the rifle stock. Hair thick and black, skin dark and faces broad, they certainly looked enough like Indians to be the real thing, Fargo noted as he raced toward the quartet pulling Caroline along the deck. One was alone to one side, and Fargo chose him first, fired a single shot, and the man half-whirled as he fell over the low rail to the deck below.

The others dragging Caroline halted, spun, and Fargo saw one start to raise a rifle. The Colt barked again and the man staggered backward as he bent in two and collapsed into a heap on the deck. The other two faced him, but they'd flung Caroline to the deck and were positioned half over her. In the darkness, his shot might well plow into Caroline.

Cursing under his breath, the Trailsman raced forward and one of the two figures came to meet him. He saw the man raise a bow, arrow already on the bowstring, and Fargo dropped to the deck as the shaft hurtled straight at him. He felt it scrape along the top of his head as he hit the deck facedown. He looked up to see the figure racing at him with a hunting knife in hand, and lying prone, he managed to bring his arm around and fire.

The heavy bullet met the onrushing figure at almost point-blank range, and Fargo saw the man's abdomen break open in a gush of red. Twisting his body to the side, Fargo just avoided the figure as it crashed facedown onto the deck.

The Trailsman pushed to his feet and saw the fourth attacker dragging Caroline down the second companionway from the deck. There was no time to reload, so he bolted forward along the narrow deck, reaching the steps to see the man halfway to the bottom with Caroline. Fargo started to race down the steps when the volley of arrows slammed into the steps on all sides of him; he twisted, flattened himself on the steps, and slid downward as another hail of arrows smashed against the companionway.

He cast a glance to the deck below and saw four attackers just about to let fly another volley of arrows. They couldn't keep missing him, he realized. He'd been damn lucky so far. He continued to slide down the steps on his stomach when he heard three pistol shots in quick succession; he grabbed hold of the stairway rail and glanced up at the deck above.

A redheaded figure was leaning over the low rail as he fired down at the attackers still on the bottom deck. Fargo pulled himself to his feet. He searched the darkness to find the figure pulling Caroline to the edge of the deck, one hand over her mouth, the other twisting her head back.

Fargo vaulted over the companionway railing and dropped to the deck below, landing on the balls of his feet and instantly breaking into a run. The attacker was pulling Caroline into a canoe that another figure held against the gunwale.

Fargo neared the edge of the boat just as the attackers pushed away in the canoe, one paddling, the other holding Caroline as she struggled to get free. He kept charging, reached the gunwale, and leapt into the air, feet first. His powerful figure hurtled through the air and came smashing down into the canoe, momentum and weight turning his body into a thundering javelin. The thin, birch-bark bottom of the canoe shattered as he plunged through it, and he glimpsed the others topple into the water.

One attacker lost his grip on Caroline and Fargo fought his way back to the surface and saw the girl swimming for the boat. But the figure splashed water hard in a stubborn pursuit. The Trailsman dived underwater, swam forward below the surface, and came up almost opposite the pursuer. He yanked the Colt from its holster. The attacker tried to turn but Fargo brought the barrel of the revolver down hard on the man's skull. The figure vanished under the surface of the water and Fargo struck out for the boat, reached the low rail just as Caroline did. His arm around her waist, he helped her up over the gunwale. She sprawled on the deck and gasped in deep breaths. She pushed herself to sit up as he came alongside her.

"You all right?" he asked.

"Thanks to you." She nodded. The pale-yellow nightgown, now thoroughly wet, clung to her round, high breasts and outlined their firm curves and tiny points as if she wore nothing.

"Hate to tear myself away," he said. "Stay here and get your breath back. I'll be back in a minute." He rose and ran toward the cargo room as other crew members appeared. He saw Ez Crawley on the deck above. A few passengers also came into sight from the upper deck as he disappeared into the cargo hold. The sacks of grain and wheat were gone, every one of them. He ran out onto the starboard side of the riverboat where the raft had been. His eyes went to the dark, deep shadows of the shoreline, but the raiders had vanished into the trees.

Fargo turned away, his lips a thin line and his head filled with racing thoughts. They had to have been moving in the trees, pacing the riverboat, waiting for their chance, certain one of the river obstacles would give it to them sooner or later. Two men carrying each canoe, four hoisting the log raft, he mused with eyes narrowed as he crossed the boat and came out on the other side. Five of the attackers lay dead on the deck, and as he strode toward the still forms, he saw that Captain Billy had come down from the pilot house, his round face drawn.

"This the way it happened the other times?" Fargo asked Billy.

"Yes." The captain nodded. "Only there were more of them this time. Guess they expected more trouble."

"They got it," a voice said at his shoulder, and Fargo turned to see the tall, red-haired figure there. "Heard the noise. Couldn't hang back this time," Canyon said with an almost apologetic grin.

Fargo glimpsed Monica looking down from the deck above. He bent low over the figure of the first slain attacker and felt the frown dig into his brow. He crossed to the second, then the third still form, and finally the last two. The frown stayed deep on his brow as he rose and met Canyon's eyes. "Indians," he grunted. "Saux Fox. No damn doubt about it."

"This kind of shoots down your theory, I'd say," Canyon observed.

"Maybe and maybe not," Fargo said, and saw Canyon's brows lift. "I still say Indians don't steal sacks of grain. It just doesn't fit."

"Maybe they're adopting some of the white man's ways, selling the grain off to other tribes just the way our outlaws sell off stolen goods," Canyon suggested.

Fargo half-shrugged, lowered his voice so only Canyon could hear it. "Let's talk more later."

"Back to the poker table," Canyon said brightly and loudly. "This interrupted a good hand." He strode off with a wave.

Fargo saw Caroline come toward him. She had gone to her cabin and come back in a cotton robe and she halted beside Captain Billy.

"Ez at the wheel?" she asked, and the captain nodded.

"I'm thinking the gambling man is right, Fargo," Billy said. "Indians who've grown real smart."

"Too smart," Fargo grunted, his eyes peering at the darkness of the riverbank.

"What are you thinking?" Caroline asked.

"They were prepared to attack. They had to be prepared to escape with the sacks. That means a lot of extra horses or a wagon. I'm betting on a wagon," Fargo said. "I want to go after them. Where can you put me ashore?"

"Go after them?" Captain Billy frowned. "Hell, you can't go after them alone. Anyway, they're gone by now."

"I'll pick up their tracks, even by dark," Fargo said. "I want to get them before they have too much of a head start."

"You can't do anything alone, 'cept get yourself killed," Billy said.

"I don't figure to do that," Fargo said. "Where can you put me ashore?"

"No place till we dock at Muscatine in the morning," the captain said. "The banks are all soft and shifting mud along this stretch of river. We can't go anywhere near them."

Fargo swore softly and felt Captain Billy's hand close onto his shoulder. "You tried, Fargo. You did your best. Maybe there'll be another time and you can really stop them," the man said.

"I want to go after them now," Fargo muttered.

Captain Billy shrugged. "You can get off at Muscatine in the morning if you've still a mind to do so." He turned to some of the crew who had come forward. "Get rid of this garbage and clean the deck. That damn sawyer's gone down. We can go now," he said, and started to climb to the wheelhouse. He paused on the steps to glance back at Fargo, his round face tired. "You did all you could, Fargo. Nobody can ask more. Leave it at that and get some sleep," he said, and went on upward.

"I think maybe he's right," Fargo heard Caroline say as he turned to her. "I thank you again, Fargo," she said, her round face grave.

"Canyon O'Grady deserves some of that thanks," Fargo said. "They had me pinned down. He gave me the chance to go after you."

"Then I'll remember to thank him," Caroline said. "But you don't think he's right about the Indians, do you? Why not?"

"The Fox aren't that smart. They're no Sioux or Crow. And I never saw Indians take the white man's ways except for drinking. But mostly it doesn't feel right inside."

"And that's what you really trust, isn't it, your feelings?"

"Guess so." He smiled. "Feelings don't lie. Sometimes we read them wrong or we twist them to fit what we want them to be. But if we read them right, they don't lie." He paused and saw her regarding him thoughtfully. "You'd best get back to bed," he said. "Next time don't be so quick to rush smack dab into the middle of a battle."

"It's called wanting to help," Caroline said.

"It's also called having too much heart and not enough head."

Her brown eyes narrowed at him. "That could almost be a compliment."

"Whatever you like." He shrugged and started to move away.

"Where are you going?" Caroline asked.

"I'm not sure."

"My cabin's yours if you want to use it."

"Not likely," he said, and saw the question flare in her eyes though she held back asking it. "I won't be going to Darlene's, either," he said.

"The thought never crossed my mind," she snapped.

"The hell it didn't." Fargo laughed and hurried away. He climbed the steps to the next deck and stepped into the gambling salon to find it empty except for Darlene and a busboy cleaning away drinks.

She saw the surprise in his face as she piled glasses on a tray. "A night like this sends folks to their cabins. They don't want to be around in case there's more trouble," she said.

"That figures."

"Will you be coming by?"

"Not tonight," he said as he backed from the salon and hurried down the corridor to the door of Canyon's cabin. The door opened at his knock and Canyon greeted him in shirt sleeves. Fargo saw Monica sitting on the edge of the bed inside the cabin. "Sorry, didn't know you had company," Fargo said.

"Come in," Canyon said, and pulled the door open wider.

"Just wanted to thank you for your help," Fargo said blandly as he stepped inside. "Hello, Monica," he added, and the young woman returned a warm smile. He turned to Canyon and let his eyes add emphasis to his words. "I'm not waiting till morning to be put ashore," he said. "It's a low deck. The Ovaro can handle it."

"Easily," Canyon agreed.

"You mean you're going to go after them tonight?" Monica's voice broke in. "You still think it's more than just Indians raiding?"

"Give the lady a cigar," Fargo said.

"You first thought they weren't real Indians, but now you know differently," Monica reminded him.

"I was wrong about that. Hired Indians instead of fake ones, but for the same end—to make it look like nothing more than Indian raids on the boat."

"You're staying with your theory that somebody's out to get Captain Billy?" Monica pressed.

"That's right. The two sets of bushwhackers that tried to kill me weren't Indians," Fargo said. Monica's nod conceded the point.

"When do you figure to be back, Fargo?" Canyon asked.

"Depends on what I find," Fargo said. "If I find a good trail, maybe not till you reach St. Louis."

"That'll only be a few days. After Muscatine, the boat has only one stop before St. Louis," Monica said.

"If you don't get back before we sail again, I'll look around for you in St. Louis," Canyon said. "Never can tell what I might stumble onto."

"I'd appreciate that, friend," Fargo said, and tossed Monica a smile. "Take good care of him," he said to her with a nod to Canyon.

"I'll try," she said pleasantly, and he hurried from the cabin. Canyon closed the door and returned to sit down beside Monica's onyx-haired sultriness.

"We won't be having any more interruptions to-night," he said.

Monica smiled. "You and Fargo have certainly be-come fast friends in a hurry," she observed.

Canyon laughed. "Sometimes happens that way," he said. "I like him. He's an exciting lad, not afraid to tackle anything." He tossed Monica a wide smile as he silently cursed her acuity.

"I like him, too," she said, and lifted her arms to encircle Canyon's neck. "But his kind can get you into trouble. I don't want to see that. I want you here taking care of me. Selfish, I know, but that's how I feel."

"Selfish, but so nice," Canyon murmured, and found Monica's warm lips on his.

"Let Fargo chase his own villains. You chase me," Monica murmured.

"That won't be hard," Canyon said as he stretched out across the bed with her and his fingers began to unbutton her gown.

6

Fargo made his way down the dark decks to the stables just before the stern of the riverboat. The Ovaro heard his approach, caught the scent of him, and whinnied before Fargo got to the corner stall and reached out to stroke the horse's powerful jet-black neck. He was running one hand down along the Ovaro's crest when he stopped in surprise. He saw the reins first, then the bit and bridle, and his eyes moved down the horse to where the saddle sat across the glistening white back and loins.

"What in hell . . ." Fargo muttered.

"I thought I'd get him ready for you," the voice said. It came from behind the stall and the compact figure stepped into sight. "I knew you'd be coming here," Caroline said. "I knew you weren't going to wait till morning to go after them."

"Smart-ass," he grunted.

"I'm ready."

"For what?"

"To go with you."

"Forget it. I go alone, honey."

"Then I'll follow. I want answers, too," Caroline

said, the edge coming into her voice, part reproof, part chiding. "If you remember, I came in handy enough last time, first saving your neck and then bringing the horses back," she said, triumph taking over her tone. She'd made her point, he admitted inwardly, but she was the kind to follow and be more of a problem that way.

"I haven't time for arguing. Get your horse," he growled. Leading the Ovaro out of the stable, he saw Caroline follow with a light-boned brown gelding. He swung onto the Ovaro on the flat space on the deck and cast a glance at Caroline. She sat her horse with calm confidence.

"Start off hard and let your horse do the jumping," Fargo said, then turned and brought his hand down hard on the Ovaro's rump. The horse leapt forward half a length across the deck, saw the raised gunwale rise up in front, and powerful hindquarter muscles knotting, lifted himself into the air. The Ovaro sailed in midair off the boat and landed hard in the river.

Fargo, legs tight, held his seat, and the horse began to paddle instantly. He looked back to see Caroline leaping from the boat, the gelding's leap not as powerful as the Ovaro's yet enough to clear the gunwale. She hit the water with a loud splash and let the horse find its swimming stride before turning to follow Fargo as he headed for the shore.

The Ovaro found footing as the bank neared and Fargo was ashore when Caroline came out on the gelding. She swung alongside him as he headed north and rode along the water's edge.

"Billy had to have heard the splashes. He'll realize what they meant," she said as they rode.

"You were right about him."

"How?"

"He's not the man I used to know. He seems to be resigned to things going bad for him," Fargo said. "He's a tired and discouraged man."

"That's why I had to fight with him to bring you into this. But even tired and discouraged people deserve help. Maybe more than most folks."

"Maybe," Fargo allowed, and cast a glance up at the sky. The moon was still behind clouds. He swore softly. He had hoped for at least the last of the moonlight, but he continued on, determined to get some kind of lead. He slowed as they went on for another half-hour and finally reined to a halt, his eyes on the riverbank where the water lapped the shore. "This is the place," he said, pointing to the long, deep marks still in the soft sandy mud of the bank. "They dragged everything up here and into the trees."

He swung to the ground and began to push his way slowly through the shore trees, mostly sandbar willow and slippery elm. He halted every few feet in the blackness and felt along the trees with his hands, changing directions when his fingers found broken twig ends and older branches that had still not snapped back in place.

The task was painfully slow and Caroline followed, holding her own horse and the Ovaro. Suddenly Fargo halted as his outstretched hands failed to touch a branch. Peering hard into the blackness, he saw the dark shapes of the trees a few feet to his left and others to the right. They had reached an oblong clear place in the trees.

Fargo dropped to one knee, moving his fingers across the ground. He uttered a snort of triumph as his hands found the deep tracks of the wagon wheels. "They had the wagon hidden away in here," he said, and rose to move slowly across the clear space as he felt along the ground with the toe of his boot in the wheel tracks. The wheel marks moved into the thicker tree cover again and he followed along carefully until he saw the trees begin to thin out some hundred yards back of the river.

He halted, a dozen yards from the relatively open land, and took the Ovaro from Caroline. "I expected we'd get the last of the moonlight, but we haven't. It'll be too slow to keep on this way. We can make up time when dawn comes," he said. "So we've a few hours to get some rest."

Caroline folded herself against a tree trunk and he stretched out on a bed of haircap moss, closing his eyes at once to make the most of the few hours' respite. He saw Caroline sleep quickly.

The few hours drifted by silently until the gray-pink streaks of dawn touched the sky. Fargo woke and saw that Caroline had fallen from against the tree and lay curled on the ground. He shook her gently and her light-brown eyes snapped open at once, a flash of panic touching her face.

"Just me," he said, and helped pull her to her feet.

"I just want to freshen up," she said, and he took the time to do the same with his own canteen.

The edge of the new sun had touched the horizon when they rode out of the heavy tree cover and onto land that was largely flat with large clusters of basswood and chinquapin oak. The wagon-wheel marks were deep in soft ground and easy to follow. They rolled north, Fargo noted, and set a steady ground-consuming pace.

Caroline stayed beside him, round, high breasts bouncing in perfect unison.

"Talk to me while we ride," he said. "About Ez Crawley."

"Ez is a hard man to like; he doesn't much like people. But he wouldn't do anything to hurt Captain Billy," Caroline said.

"How do you know that?"

"Because Billy's been the one person who's been good to him all these years. Billy stuck with him when nobody else would put up with his surliness."

"That's nice," Fargo said laconically. "But it's all nice warm feeling. Knowing is something else."

"I don't know, as you put it. But I certainly believe that. Don't you ever believe in anyone?"

"I believe people change. They get into trouble. They need money. And sometimes they nurse hates nobody ever suspects. I don't rule out anybody. Money can make people do all kinds of things."

"Why rule me out, then?"

"I wouldn't," Fargo said, and met her quick glare. "Except for one thing," he added blandly.

"What's that?"

"You brought me. I don't think you'd do that to get yourself caught," he said, and saw the anger slide from her face.

"You do have your own way of looking at things," she allowed. "But then I found that out already," she added tartly. He smiled for he knew she wasn't referring just to the raids. "And I don't believe Ez would do anything to hurt Captain Billy," she finished, and fell silent as they rode.

Fargo continued to follow the wagon-wheel trail, but his eyes took in the unshod pony prints that accompanied the wheel marks. Six riders, he counted, and probably two more on the wagon. The prints moved down a path onto a low plateau and ran alongside a lone line of oaks. He caught the flash of sunlight on water through the trees at his right and glimpsed another to the distant left.

"We're getting close to Minnesota Territory," he said.

"Because of the lakes?" Caroline asked.

"That's right." He nodded. "The Indians call the Minnesota Territory the place where the sky is in the land because of all the lakes." He moved sideways with the pinto as the trails reached the end of the line of oaks. He saw the nearest lake come fully into view—a large, irregularly shaped circle. The tracks moved alongside the nearest shore of the lake and continued on only a few feet from the water.

Fargo leaned over in the saddle as he studied the trail. He suddenly reined to a halt, raised one arm, and saw Caroline rein up behind him as he swung from the saddle, his eyes fastened on the ground. "They stopped here and met another wagon." He pointed to the marks on the ground and scanned the new hoofprints beside the second wagon. "Two riders with it. No Fox. Horses with shoes," he muttered.

"What's it mean?"

"I don't know. Maybe they transferred the sacks to the second wagon," Fargo said. "And maybe they didn't."

"Which do we follow?"

Fargo's lips pulled back in a grimace as he tossed the question in his mind. "The wagon we've been tailing. Maybe the sacks were transferred, but maybe they weren't. I want to see where those Indians are headed," he said. "If I guess wrong, we double back and pick up the tracks of the other wagon." He pulled himself onto the Ovaro and put the horse into a fast canter as he followed along the one set of wagon tracks that moved along the edge of the lake and finally went on straight north.

Even at a fast canter, with only one stop to rest the horses, he had ridden another two hours before he slowed as the wagon-wheel tracks moved down a passage between rock outcroppings. He glanced at Caroline again, saw the strain on her round-cheeked face and the determination that accompanied it. Her natural feistiness gave her strength most women couldn't draw upon. He saw her follow him as he sent the pinto up a low hill, picked his way among rocks, and halted where he could look down at the terrain below.

He spotted the wagon some hundred yards beyond and below. It was an old, battered farm wagon with an open top that let him quickly see there were no sacks of grain inside it. He frowned and moved his eyes to the ground near the wagon. There he saw the eight figures scattered around the wagon, motionless figures with arms and legs outspread, a few on their sides, some facedown.

"My God," he heard Caroline gasp. "They've all been killed, and there's nothing in the wagon."

Fargo's jaw throbbed as he stared at the figures, Caroline's words an echo of his own thoughts. "I want a closer look. You can stay here," he said.

"No, I'm coming with you," she said, and followed him down to the small dip of land. She halted a few paces behind as he dismounted and stepped to the first half-naked form. He bent down over the Indian, rose, and strode to the next one and then the next. He turned the fourth Indian onto his back before he straightened up.

"Shit," Fargo bit out, and glanced at Caroline. "They're not dead. They're drunk," he snapped, and saw Caroline's lips fall open. He strode to the wagon, reached one leg beneath it, and kicked. A wooden cask rolled out to rock back and forth on the ground. He glanced at the perimeter of the circle of figures and spotted two more empty casks, with another split open. He brought his eyes back to the silent, motionless forms.

"Bastards," he muttered. "They've drunk themselves into a blind stupor. They'll be unconscious for hours, maybe half the day." He spun on his heel and crossed to the Ovaro. "We can't wait around for that. I guessed wrong. They did transfer the sacks. Let's move," he said as he climbed onto the horse. He set off at a fast pace and Caroline stayed with him as he raced back to the lake and the second set of wagon tracks.

He slowed finally, aware that he was pushing the horses too hard, and he halted when they reached the lake to let the horses stand in the water to their ankles while they drank.

"You were right. Hired Indians," Caroline said as she stood beside him.

"Hired with whiskey, sure-fire payment for Indians like the Fox," Fargo said, and Caroline's glance questioned. "Tribes with nothing left but to live in the white man's shadow. They're happy to drink the world away whenever they can."

"Hired to make it all look as if it were only random Indian raids. You were right about all of it," Caroline said.

"Hooray for me. But that doesn't help Captain Billy.

We have to get the sacks back so he's off the hook for the grain. When we do that, I expect we'll find out who's back of it," Fargo said.

"Got any ideas on that?"

"No. Could be anybody anywhere, maybe somebody you don't know at all, someone who knows Captain Billy's strapped from his gambling."

Caroline nodded, her round-cheeked face grave. "I'm afraid suddenly. If we catch up to them, they're not just going to turn the grain over to us."

"I don't expect they will. But that's my department."

Her hands came up to press against his chest. "I asked you to come to help Billy. I don't want you killed over it. I guess I didn't think far enough."

"You didn't," he said grimly. "Wheels start to roll, they keep on. Get your horse."

She reached up and her lips brushed his cheek, a soft, fluttery kiss, quick and light as a butterfly's touch. She hurried to the gelding and climbed into the saddle.

Fargo set a steady pace. The wagon tracks went west this time, across low hills in the lengthening shadows of the afternoon. When the tracks finally led down into an uneven stretch of land, he moved the Ovaro up behind a low rise, Caroline at his heels. He drew to a halt when a house came into view, tar-roofed, with a long extra section built onto the rear. The wagon, another open-topped farm wagon, rested unhitched to one side of the house, and Fargo saw the two horses tethered nearby.

"It's empty," Caroline breathed.

"They had plenty of time to carry the sacks into the house," Fargo said. "We'll take a look."

"How are we going to do that?"

"If you can't get into the fox's den, you make the fox come out."

"How?"

"Bait," he answered, and her eyes narrowed at him.

"Bait meaning me."

"You insisted on coming along. You said you could help." Fargo shrugged.

"What do I do?"

"Ride up to the house. They'll see you and come outside to meet you. That's all I need," Fargo said. "The important thing is that you keep yourself away from them. Don't let them get close to you."

"I understand."

"Give me five minutes and then start down," Fargo said, drew the big Sharps from its saddle holster, and moved forward on foot. He scurried across the low hill from oak to oak until he found a knoll that gave him a clear, close view of the house. He positioned himself and he had counted off a little over five minutes when he saw Caroline appear on the brown gelding. She walked the horse toward the house and hadn't reached the front yet when the door opened and two men hurried out, guns in hand.

"That's far enough, girlie," one growled.

Caroline halted. "I'm lost. I need some directions," she said.

"What are you doing out in this country all by yourself, sweetie?" the man asked, and slid his gun back into the holster. The other holstered his weapon also.

Fargo's eyes swept the two figures. The taller one wore a scraggly mustache and the other one had a pudgy, soft nose in a pudgy face.

"I wasn't by myself," Fargo heard Caroline say.

"There were three of us. We saw some Indians and separated to draw less attention to ourselves. I got lost afterward. I'm trying to reach Minnesota Territory."

She was giving out a good story, a touch of helplessness in her voice, but the two men started toward her, separating to step to both sides of the horse.

"Get down and rest a spell, honey," the mustached one said, and the other nodded eagerly.

Fargo swept both with another glance. Neither seemed too bright. Hired hands, he grunted, but that's what he'd expected.

"Thank you, but I don't have time to stay," Caroline said, and backed the gelding as the two men advanced on her.

Fargo brought the rifle to his chin, steadied the barrel on a knob of rock. He was about to call out when the voice cut him off and he saw the third figure step from around the back of the house, six-gun in hand.

"That's enough goin' backward, girlie," the man said, a short-legged figure with a square, piggish face. Caroline halted, her eyes on the gun in the man's hand. "Get off the horse now," the man ordered with abrupt harshness.

Fargo swore silently. He wanted at least one alive to answer questions. But he couldn't let them get their hands on Caroline. He'd be out of options, then, and they'd have the advantage. The third man stepped forward with sudden quickness and Fargo cursed silently again. He was out of time and options, and he shifted the rifle a fraction of an inch and fired. The man had started to reach up to Caroline when his feet left the ground as he flew backward to smash into the ground on his back.

Fargo saw Caroline fling herself low across the gelding's neck as he fired the rifle again. This time the pudgy-nosed figure spun completely around, both hands clasped to his chest, took another half-turn, and collapsed.

The third man was streaking toward the horses and Fargo rose to his feet. "Hold it," he shouted. "I want to talk." But the man continued to race for the horses. "Some answers and you walk away alive," Fargo shouted again, but the man vaulted onto the nearest horse, snapped the reins loose, and streaked for the back of the house. "Goddamn," Fargo swore aloud as he spun and ran to where the Ovaro waited. He hit the saddle without slowing even a half-pace, the rifle still clutched in his right hand. Digging heels into the horse, he sent the pinto racing down the low hill to the house. "Stay here," he yelled at Caroline as he charged past her and on around the house.

He instantly saw where the third man had cut through tall brush and a cluster of white-flowered sweet clover. He sent the pinto after the fleeing horse and rider and saw that the man was bent on running, not covering tracks. He possibly thought he wouldn't be chased and he stayed in the high brush as he raced away. Fargo followed and charged through brush already partially flattened and guessed he gained close to a minute by that.

He emerged from the brush onto open land and glimpsed the fleeing rider disappear over a low rise. He let the Ovaro go full out now, and the gleaming black-and-white horse flew across the ground on pounding hooves. He went over the rise and saw the man again.

This time the rider half-turned in the saddle to see

him. The man drew his gun and fired, wild shots that wasted bullets and time.

Fargo pushed the big Sharps back into the saddle holster. He saw the man race on, swerve, and send his horse down a narrow passage that led into a long ravine. From where he rode, Fargo could see that the ravine could be entered by another half-dozen passages farther on, and he sent the pinto racing forward full out. He saw down into the ravine: the fleeing rider had halted, turned, gun ready to fire as he waited for his pursuer to charge out of the passage.

But Fargo was already twenty yards beyond when he swerved the pinto down through one of the other passages. The man had begun to race forward again when the big pinto charged out in front of him by some fifteen yards. He reined up, an automatic reaction, and brought his gun up to fire, but Fargo had his Colt in hand. He aimed, fired, and the man clutched at his left shoulder before he dropped from his horse. He hit the ground and lay still.

Fargo slowed the Ovaro as he approached the figure. "Talk and you can still ride out of here alive," Fargo said, but the figure lay still. The Trailsman holstered the Colt and started to swing from the saddle when the man's head lifted, his lips drawn back in a grimace of pain. But the hand under his chest clutched the six-gun and Fargo flung himself forward as the shot exploded and barely missed his head. Fargo hit the ground rolling and glimpsed the man fire another shot from his prone position, the hand holding his gun soaked red with blood pouring from his shoulder.

Fargo yanked the Colt from its holster as he rolled again and came up on one knee. The man was trying to bring his gun hand out farther from his chest; he had managed to half-rise when Fargo's shot exploded. The man's face disappeared in a red shower of blood, bone, and flesh.

Fargo grimaced as he rose and dropped the Colt back in its holster. "Damn fool," he muttered as he turned away and climbed onto the Ovaro. The man would reveal nothing, not ever. None of them would. But they'd not be warning anyone, and perhaps that was a small victory. Too small.

Fargo's thoughts were still whirling in all directions when he returned to the house.

Caroline was still atop the gelding as he halted beside her. "You catch him?"

"I did, but he insisted on shooting instead of talking," Fargo said. "You go inside?"

"No. I was afraid. I stayed right in the saddle in case I had to run."

"Then let's have a look inside," Fargo said, and swung to the ground.

Caroline slid from the gelding and hurried after him as he strode to the house, pushed the door open, and stepped inside to find himself in a large room. A table with three coffee mugs on it stood in the center of the room, three shovels occupied one corner, a narrow cot another corner. Two mattresses were scattered on the floor along with piles of clothes. A long shelf holding some cooking utensils and a small iron stove rested against one of the walls. There were no sacks of grain anywhere.

He exchanged a grim glance with Caroline as he moved toward a burlap curtain that hung across one end of the room. His hand on the butt of the Colt at his side, he pulled the burlap back and faced the extension onto the house. A neat stack of whiskey cases was piled across the half-room.

"Where are the grain sacks?" Caroline frowned.

"Not here, that's damn plain enough. And they never were here," Fargo said. "They keep the payment whiskey casks here and take them in the wagon to wherever they're meeting the Fox," he finished.

"Then where are the grain sacks? We know they took them from the boat."

"I don't know," Fargo answered honestly.

"They must have met someone else along the way and turned the sacks over to them," Caroline said.

"No, I'd have seen the tracks. The Fox didn't meet anyone until they met the whiskey wagon for their pay."

"Sacks of grain just don't vanish into thin air," Caroline protested.

"No, they don't. Only these seem to have," Fargo said.

Caroline blinked as she stared back at him and realized she had no better answer.

7

"Are you out of your mind coming here, Fullerton? Lord Upshaw could have been here. We know we're being watched."

"I was careful."

"If you're seen coming here and then followed, it could blow everything wide open."

"Nobody saw me. Hell, it's midnight. Besides, I'm thinking everything's blown anyway.'

"What do you mean by that?"

"There was no signal from the boat last night. That means she'll dock at St. Louis with no shipment for us."

"Again?"

"That's right, again. Soon as I saw there was no signal, I took off for here."

"A fool thing to do."

"Fool or not, I'm here."

"The gold may be being held in Canada. Washington may have too many troops patrolling, looking for it. I told you, we have to be very careful. They'll come through. Just be patient."

"Something's wrong. I feel it in my bones. You've

an agent on board the boat who's supposed to signal us. Contact him and let him find out what the hell's going on."

"All right, all right, I'll get word to the boat."

"Have him contact me directly. This has to be straightened out, whatever it is."

"I'll do it. Now get out of here, for God's sake, before you're seen."

The man's bushy black eyebrows frowned as he grunted and slipped out of the side door of the town house. He stayed in the deep shadows as he hurried through the night.

Dockside at St. Louis was always a busy place. There was room for more than one riverboat to dock at once and the *Shady Lady* shared the long, wooden pier with the *Delta Queen* from New Orleans. Big dead-axle drays and Owensboro stake-sided rigs moved back and forth along with smaller and lighter Studebaker baggage wagons and merchandise trucks. Stevedores and loaders scurried about like so many grimy ants among passengers dressed in fancy silks and suits.

The red-haired figure watched from one side, leaned on one of the bollards alongside the riverboat. His eyes carefully took in the entire panorama of the dock, paused upon an attractive young woman beside a flower cart, when the voice interrupted his musings.

"There you are. I thought you were going shopping with me," it said, and Canyon O'Grady turned to see Monica coming toward him. A pale-yellow dress that hugged her hips and cupped her breasts made her black hair and black eyebrows even more intense than usual.

"God, you're a beautiful creature," Canyon marveled. "But you go on by yourself. You'll get much more shopping done than with me tagging along."

Monica paused beside him and fastened a narrow sidelong glance at him. "You're not staying back for that reason," she said. "Don't play games with me, Canyon O'Grady."

He shrugged. "Caught red-handed," he said, and tossed her a smile of dazzling charm. Monica's cool glance didn't soften. "If Fargo were here, he'd be out here having a look for himself. I just thought I'd do it for him."

"He chose to go splashing off in the night after the Indians. That's his decision. I don't see why you're so eager to involve yourself in his problem," Monica said. "You promised me you wouldn't."

"When you come back from shopping we'll have the rest of the day to ourselves," Canyon said soothingly, and again saw Monica's coolness stay firmly in place.

"I thought you understood how I felt about this. We'll talk about it when I come back," she said.

"Of course," Canyon said, and watched her stride away, anger in the way she swung her hips. He'd have to repair fences, he thought. The depths of her feelings surprised him. And pleased him, he admitted. It showed she really cared; she worried about him getting into more than he'd bargained for. He smiled. He couldn't tell her he was an expert in just that. Or that he was helping Fargo because he hadn't been able to find a damn thing out on his own assignment. Not yet, Canyon thought. But soon. Monica's caring deserved honesty. Soon, he echoed, as he returned his gaze to the teeming dockside.

Fargo had told him the grain sacks were consigned to Fullerton Haulage, and he scanned the scene again, his eyes on the wagons that rumbled their way along the dock with cargoes they had picked up. Sam's Shipping, he read on one. Healy Transport, another proclaimed. He scanned Carter Hauling, Murphy Brothers Freight, the St. Louis Wagon Company, and a half-dozen more, but no Fullerton Haulage. That was the one outfit that hadn't appeared to pick up their shipment. A frown creased his brow. Common sense dictated they'd appear to pick up the shipment consigned to them. They had no way of knowing it had been stolen in the Indian raid.

His brow still furrowed, he sauntered down the dock to the wide cobblestoned street and saw a small shed with the word DOCKMASTER over the door and a portly man seated on a high stool in front of it. " 'Morning," Canyon called out cheerfully. "I was to meet a Fullerton Haulage Company wagon. You know anything about them?"

"Fullerton?" The dockmaster frowned. "Oh, that's the new outfit."

"New?" Canyon echoed.

"Around here, anyway. They rented a warehouse a few months ago at the end of Front Street."

"Much obliged." Canyon nodded and sauntered down the long, winding street that bordered the river. He finally reached the end and saw the modest, square structure. A sign, FULLERTON HAULAGE, hung over the front door. O'Grady pushed the narrow door in to find himself in a cubbyhole of an office. A young man, not much beyond his teens, Canyon guessed, sat with obvious boredom behind a chipped wooden desk.

"Yes, sir?" he said.

"I must have missed your wagon at dockside." Canyon smiled. "I just came off the *Shady Lady.* Guess you're wondering what happened to this shipment?"

"Shipment?" The boy frowned.

"The shipment of grain," Canyon said, and saw the uncertainty stay in the boy's face.

"I don't know anything about that."

"How long have you been working here?" Canyon queried.

"Since Mr. Fullerton opened up shop."

"What about the other shipments?" Canyon probed. "You know what happened to them, don't you?"

"Other shipments? No, sir," the boy said, and Canyon decided he was being truthful. "Mr. Fullerton would know, I guess, but he's away."

"And you didn't send a wagon to the dock this morning to pick up a shipment of grain sacks?" O'Grady frowned.

"No, sir. I'd have known that. I've been here all morning," the young man answered.

"And nobody ever told you about other shipments that didn't arrive over the past month?"

"No, sir."

"Nobody ever went to the boat and filed any claims over missing shipments?" Canyon continued to press.

"Not that I heard about. Maybe you ought to talk to Jake and Sam."

"Who're they?" Canyon asked.

"Jake Brant and Sam Radar. They're Mr. Fullerton's right-hand men," the boy said. "They'll be back later."

"Thanks," Canyon said, and left the office. Outside, he strolled to the corner of the warehouse, his eyes narrowed in thought. Fullerton Haulage hadn't sent a wagon to the boat. That fact alone simmered. It didn't fit, unless they knew the grain shipment wouldn't be there. But even more strange was the obvious fact that they hadn't filed a claim for any of the other shipments that hadn't arrived.

Canyon grimaced as he sauntered along the side of the warehouse, turned the corner at the rear, and saw a pair of wide doors. Unformed thoughts gnawing at him, he pushed at one of the doors; it moved at his touch. He pulled it open wide enough to slip inside the warehouse, where he swept the interior with a quick glance.

The place was completely empty, from wall to wall and corner to corner. Not a box, not a barrel, not a carton, disturbed the emptiness. Canyon moved along the wall, eyes on the floor as he paused in each corner and scanned every inch of the board floor. Not a piece of string left over, not a shred of torn cardboard, not a broken length of crate wood, not a trace of sawdust or a sign of scuff marks on the floor met his searching gaze. He made his way back to the doors, surveyed the empty warehouse again for anything he might have missed, and then slipped back outside. Either Fullerton Haulage had stored damn little in their warehouse or they were the neatest housekeepers in the business. Canyon was pretty damn certain which was the right choice.

He turned thoughts in his mind as he sauntered back to the boat. The visit had brought no answers, but it had certainly brought more questions. He went to his cabin, shed his jacket, and lay across the bed. Fargo felt certain the raids were a cover to push Captain Billy into a hole. Where did Fullerton Haulage fit in? If they were part of the scheme, they certainly should've filed claims for the missing shipments. And if they weren't part of it, they still should've filed claims as any ordinary haulage outfit would. But they hadn't, and that didn't make any sense from either position. Canyon realized he was impatient for Fargo to return, and he wondered what he'd uncovered in his chase.

The visit to the Fullerton operation had left O'Grady with undefined, nagging unease, as though he had found something more than he had and couldn't fit it anywhere. Perhaps Fargo would return with something to tie it in. Canyon frowned and pushed away thoughts as he swung from the bed. Monica should have returned by now, but she hadn't come calling to show off her new purchases. He let a long sigh escape his lips. Pique. Monica's way of showing her displeasure with him. It was time to repair fences, the emotional kind. Women, he grunted as he walked from the cabin. They chose the damnedest times to indulge their moods, even the usually calm and sensible ones such as Monica. He hurried down the corridor to her cabin and knocked.

She opened the door and he saw she had changed from the yellow dress to a white shirt and Levi's, but the coolness was still in her face. "I expected you'd stop by," he offered.

"I expected you'd keep your word," she returned stiffly.

He smiled, stepped into the cabin, and pushed the door closed with his feet. He put his hands on his shoulders. "I did, too," he said. *"Mea culpa,"* he added, and drew a questioning frown. "Latin for, My fault, all my doing. Echoes of my old Jesuit schooling."

Monica's eyes fastened him with a long, appraising stare. "You're a fascinating man, Canyon O'Grady.

It's hard to stay angry at a gambling man who quotes Latin," she said. He pressed his mouth to hers and felt her instant response, lips softening, opening, pressing back, until she pulled away and drew stiffness back into her lovely face. "And you've entirely too much charm. But I haven't changed my feelings. It's Fargo's show. Let it stay that way."

"After I tell him a few things I found out," Canyon said. "Damn strange things, they were."

"Such as?" Monica asked, and he told her what he had learned. When he finished, her smooth brow was knit as she stared at him.

"You went to the Fullerton warehouse?" she echoed incredulously. "Why in heaven's name would you do that?"

"I got hold of something and followed it through. Seemed the logical thing to do," Canyon said, remembering to play the role of an amateur busybody.

"God, this gets worse," Monica said, plainly upset. She stared into space for a moment, then came to him, hands pressed against his chest. "Please, Canyon, don't get in any deeper. Don't go near that place again."

"Don't worry, lass," Canyon said soothingly. "I'll pass everything I've learned over to Fargo."

Monica's arms slid around his neck. "I've plans for us. I want you around to share them."

"Meanwhile, we could do some sharing now," Canyon said as his hand curled around one soft breast.

Monica nodded as she lay back onto the bed with him.

The boy stammered out answers as the two men glared furiously at him. "I didn't tell him anything. I don't know anything," he said.

"The kid's right, Jake," the short, thick-chested man said. "There's nothing he could tell."

Jake Brant grimaced out of a face made of heavy folds and thick lips, and a short, grunting sound conceded the point. "What brought him sniffing around here?" he asked the boy. "He tell you that?"

"He said there was some shipment due and he wondered why we hadn't picked it up," the boy said. "I told him I didn't know anything about any shipment. I told him to come back and talk to you."

"He say who he was?" Jake Brant barked.

"No," the boy said.

"It had to be that varmint they brought aboard to stop some Indian raids," Sam Radar put in.

"Fargo," Jake growled. "Mr. Fullerton said he was the kind that could get in the way."

"What'd he look like?" Sam asked the boy.

"Big, tall, dressed sharp, red hair," the boy said.

"Now we know what he looks like. The rest will be easy," Sam said to Jake.

"Meaning what?" Jake frowned.

"We take care of him. No more Fargo, no more digging around, no more questions. Mr. Fullerton won't be back till tomorrow and the boat starts upriver tonight. We can't wait," Sam said. "We go aboard and finish him."

"Mr. Fullerton will be real happy when we tell him we got rid of Fargo," Jake said.

"Happy enough to give us a bonus, maybe," Sam said. "We wait till dark, just before she sails. Then we go aboard, find him, and pick the right time and place."

Jake nodded and settled down in a corner of the

tiny office, anticipation showing itself through the folds of his face.

Caroline faced Fargo with her hands on her hips. "Where are the grain sacks? You know they can't just vanish. You must have some idea."

"None that adds up to anything."

"I know where they are," Caroline said excitedly. "Back in the trees and heavy brush by the riverbank where they pulled the canoes out of the water. They hid them there."

"Why? They had the wagon there to take them away," Fargo returned.

Caroline frowned for a moment and then, caught up in her own theory, exploded her answer. "That's what they wanted anyone following to think. It worked. That's exactly what we thought. It was pitch-black back there and we found the wagon tracks and followed. Only the sacks weren't in the wagon. They were hidden away in the trees and brush."

Fargo made a wry face. "Seems awful fancy for a band of whiskey-happy Indians."

"You have any better ideas?"

"No, I don't," Fargo admitted. "Let's go have a look." As Caroline hurried to mount, he cast a glance at the thickening dusk. "We'll ride a ways, then bed down for the night. We can use the rest, and that way we'll reach the river when it's still light tomorrow," he said, and led the way from the cabin as the night quickly closed in. A moon appeared and afforded a pale light as they made their way across the low hill country. Fargo found a spot to stay the night under a rocky ledge with good sweet-smelling red cedar on both sides. He offered Caroline some hardtack he kept in his saddlebag.

"I must be awfully hungry," she said as she chewed and sat beside him. "I hate this stuff."

"It's made for the body, not the soul," he said.

She finished and leaned back, her round breasts pressing beautifully against the shirt she wore. "This has turned into a lot more than I thought it would," Caroline murmured.

"Things have a way of doing that," he said, stretched, and rose. He took down his bedroll and set it out as she watched. He paused to glance at her. "Want a blanket?" he asked.

"The edge of your bedroll will be enough," she said, and her eyes stayed on him as he undressed down to his underdrawers and lay down on the bedroll at one side.

Caroline sat up, put her back to him, and slid off her skirt first, revealing a half-slip under it, then she shrugged the shirt off and made it into a thin band around her breasts. She turned and lay down on the bedroll and he took in broad, rounded shoulders and a flat, smooth midriff, the half-slip revealing nicely turned calves. "Good night, Fargo," she said.

"Good night," he answered. "By the way, thanks for that butterfly kiss yesterday."

"You making fun?" she bristled at once.

"No, not at all. Sweetness has its own way."

She turned quickly, leaned over, and brushed his cheek again with her lips, the same soft, fluttery touch, and quickly returned to her side of the bedroll. "Good night," she murmured again, and closed her eyes at once.

Fargo took a moment to enjoy the loveliness of her

breasts under the rolled-up shirt, the snub-nosed prettiness of her, and he marveled how she combined being a little girl and a woman at the same time. It was a combination she hadn't come to terms with herself yet, he realized as he turned on his side and let sleep sweep over him.

When morning came, he set a steady pace that let Caroline stay with him without exhausting the gelding. "Finding the sacks will be only a beginning. We still have to find where they hid the others and who's behind it," she said.

"Don't count chickens until," Fargo grunted.

"You don't think the sacks will be there, do you?"

"I wouldn't put a lot of money on it."

"They have to be there," Caroline insisted. "They didn't have them, and you said yourself they hadn't met anyone along the way."

"I know what I said! And I know what I can't put together. For now, we ride and stop guessing."

Caroline fell silent and he retraced steps, picking up the original set of wagon tracks they had followed from the riverbank. He halted when they reached the edge of the irregularly shaped lake and he peered down at the tracks, still clear near the shore. "This is where they met the wagon with the whiskey."

"And didn't transfer the sacks," Caroline said.

He swept the prints on the ground again and swore silently. No sign to help him, nothing but the two sets of wagon tracks. He sent the Ovaro forward again, grimness in his face.

The day had slipped into the afternoon, the sun lowering across the distant sky, when he saw the winding ribbon that was the Mississippi as he crested a rise. Another half-hour brought him to the thick bank of willows and slippery elm. He slowed to a walk as he began to push his way through the trees, Caroline at his heels, until he halted and slid to the ground. The wagon prints were still clear in the soft earth.

"Start searching," he muttered to Caroline as he began to push back the thick brush and low foliage.

Scouring the area with Caroline helping, he finally turned to her and met her wide-eyed gaze. "Nothing," he said flatly.

"Somebody else could've come and taken them. There's been plenty of time," she countered with a half-shrug.

"There has been; only that didn't happen. The sacks were never left here. Heavy sacks would've flattened down brush and grass. There's not a mark, not an indentation. They were never left in the brush."

"You're saying they were put in the wagon."

"I'm saying they weren't left in the brush and I think they were put in the wagon. That's why it was here," he answered.

"Then where are they? What happened to them?"

Fargo grimaced. "I've no answers on that, not for me and not for you," he said, and threw a glance skyward where the sun had disappeared beneath the horizon. "Where's the *Shady Lady* now?"

"Sailing upriver. She won't put in till Keokuk in the morning," Caroline said.

"Then we can catch her from here."

"Sure. Before midnight, I'd guess."

"Let's move. We give a repeat performance. I'll swim aboard tonight and you take the horses to Keokuk and board in the morning."

"Why? What do you expect to find out?" Caroline queried.

"I want to see if anything goes on while folks think I'm off chasing Indians."

"Goes on with whom?"

"Anybody and everybody."

"Mostly Ez Crawley?" she suggested.

"He's one."

"Darlene?" she slid at him with a waspish edge.

"She's included," Fargo said. "Somebody on the boat makes contact with someone on shore. Information is passed, plans are put into action. Maybe it's done by personal contact but maybe there's a signal sent from the boat. I don't know and I'm not ruling out anything. I just want to be aboard without anyone knowing it and keep watch till morning."

Caroline nodded and fell in beside him as he set off parallel to the river. The land rose. The best path turned inland for a few miles but generally moved north. He stayed on it, though the river fell from sight. His eyes moved to a crest to his right after they'd gone on another mile or so, and he saw two horsemen peering down at them. The two men kept pace for a few hundred yards and then disappeared down the other side of the crest.

Fargo slowed. "Stay here," he said to Caroline as he spurred the pinto up the hill to the top and halted at the crest. His gaze swept the other side of the hill and the land below, but the two horsemen had disappeared. No real problem with a little fast riding and the thick tree cover below, Fargo mused. And nothing alarming of itself, he realized, returning down the hillside to Caroline.

"I take it you didn't see anything much," she said, and he nodded agreement.

"Just being careful." He stepped up the pace again

and the day began to wear to an end when they came in sight of a small shack a few hundred feet below in a dip of land. He slowed as they came abreast of the shack and he saw the figure of a man lying facedown in the yard in front of the house. A few chickens and a pig wandered loose through a broken fence, but the figure didn't stir.

"Something's wrong with that man," Caroline said, and reined to a halt.

"Looks that way," Fargo said. "But we don't have time to find out."

"Of course we have time. Maybe he fell. Maybe he's hurt or had a heart attack."

"Keep riding," Fargo said. He started to move forward but halted as Caroline stayed in place.

"I'll do no such thing. A man's hurt or sick. It wouldn't be right to just ride on."

"Probably not, but that's what we're going to do."

Caroline frowned at him with a mixture of anger and incomprehension in her eyes. "I don't understand you, Fargo. You put your life on the line to help me and Captain Billy, but you won't take five minutes to help that poor man."

"I'm full of contradictions. Ride," he growled.

"No," she snapped, wheeled the horse, and sent the gelding plunging down to the shack.

"Dammit, come back here," he yelled after her, but she had already reached the bottom. He saw her jump from the horse and go to the prone figure. She knelt down beside the man and had bent lower to peer at him when Fargo saw the man's arms come up, wrap around Caroline, and pull her on top of him. He heard Caroline's scream of surprise over his own curse. The man rolled Caroline onto her back, brought his knees

129

up, and pushed himself to his feet while keeping his grip on the girl.

Fargo, his mouth a thin line, watched two other figures stroll from inside the shack, rifles in hand.

"Get down here, mister," one called out, and Fargo swore under his breath as he slowly moved the pinto down the slope to the house. He took in the two men first, the same ones he'd seen on the crest of land. He grunted silently and shifted his glance to Caroline.

Her wide, round eyes held apology along with fear while the man behind her, a big, powerful figure with an unkempt beard, held one arm around her waist, the other across her breasts.

"Get off the horse," one of the other two ordered, and motioned with his rifle, an army-issue Spencer carbine.

Fargo swung to the ground and measured the carbine aimed at his stomach. Even a child couldn't miss at so close a range. He cursed silently as the other man pulled the Colt from him.

"Turn around," the other ordered. " 'Less you like seeing your head stove in."

Fargo turned his back to the two men, every muscle in his body tensed. There was no avoiding what was about to happen. There was only the slender chance to lessen the results. Feeling more than listening, the hairs on the back of his neck responding to the swish of air currents, he felt the man take a step closer, felt his hand come down with the pistol butt. Fargo braced himself and turned his head a fraction to the left so that the blow didn't land squarely with full force. Even so, it was powerful enough, and flashing lights exploded inside his head as he pitched forward.

The Trailsman felt himself hit the ground, his head

still filled with flashes of colored lights as it throbbed. But he wasn't unconscious, as he would have been had the blow struck squarely. He lay still. Dimly, as if from a faraway place, he heard the sound of laughter and footsteps turning away. He didn't dare move yet or try to shake his head, and the lights continued to flash on and off inside him. The throbbing became a focused pain along the side of his skull. But the flashing lights blinked off and the world began to swim back in place. Sounds took on clarity and he heard Caroline's voice, half-screamed sobs, and the harsh laughter of the three men. He lifted his head, turned to see the three of them had her pinned against the fence of a small pen as they were busy running hands over her, yanking at her clothes.

Their concentration was all on Caroline. Fargo rose quietly to one knee, caught sight of a pitchfork resting against a stump not more than six feet away. He'd have to hit fast and hard, do as much damage as he could before one of them had a chance to draw his gun. Fargo reached to the calf holster around his leg and drew the thin, double-edged throwing knife sometimes called an Arkansas toothpick. He took aim as Caroline's screams grew louder; he chose the big one with the unkempt beard, whose back all but hid Caroline's body. Tossing the blade with all his strength, he saw it hurtle through the air and slam into the back of the man's neck with such force that only the hilt against the folds of his skin stopped it from going all the way through.

Fargo saw the figure stiffen and stagger backward, but he was already racing the few feet to the pitchfork. The other two were still not aware of what had happened as they swarmed over Caroline. He chose the one to the right and charged, the pitchfork held lancelike in front of him. He saw one of the other two turn to look at the bearded one as he dropped to his knees and swayed, the hilt of the knife still protruding from the back of his thick neck. The second man turned further, his eyes opening wide as he saw the charging figure coming at him. He tried to reach his gun, but he was too late. The three prongs of the pitchfork hurtled into him, the lower prong piercing his abdomen, the middle one his chest, and the third his throat.

Fargo dropped his hold on the handle of the pitchfork and the man hung impaled, quivering soundlessly. The Trailsman had already twisted and dived down to his left to slam into the third man's ankles as two shots just missed his back.

The man, almost upended, lost balance and fell forward, firing another shot harmlessly into the ground. Fargo reached out, closed one hand around the man's ankle, and pulled. The man toppled sideways, his finger automatically tightening on the trigger to send another shot wildly into the air. He tried to twist onto his back and bring his gun around, but Fargo was on him, one hand closing around his wrist and forcing his arm back. At the same time, Fargo's forearm came down with all his weight behind it and slammed into the man's throat. The man's mouth flew open in a gagging, gargling sound. Fargo felt the small bones and ligaments of the trachea collapse. He rolled away, pushed to his feet as the man twitched spasmodically and a pinkish liquid began to stain his lips.

Fargo looked away and found Caroline on one knee, pulling her shirt closed before she stood up. He stepped toward her and she rose and rushed to him, burying her head into his chest.

"Oh, God, I'm sorry, I'm sorry," she half-sobbed. She stayed against him as, one arm around her waist, he led her to the gelding.

"Mount up. We've riding to do," he said firmly, and she raised her brown eyes to him, searched his face with wonderment as he retrieved his Colt.

"You knew," she murmured. "How? How did you know?"

"Something you develop, a sense of things, of rightness and wrongness. I can't explain it, but it's real. The first two riders saw us from the crest. When I went up to look for them, they'd disappeared. That meant they went off riding hard. With no real reason," he said. "Nothing wrong in that of itself, but then we come to that shack and a man's lying there in need of help. It was a shade too neat. I wasn't sure, mind you, but it didn't feel right."

"And I wouldn't listen," Caroline said with despair. "I had to be the Good Samaritan."

"I wouldn't tell you to change, honey," Fargo said. "Just listen more."

She stayed against him and suddenly reached up, her lips finding his, soft, sweet, clinging for a long moment, then pulling away. "Thank you, Fargo," she murmured.

"What happened to the butterfly kiss?" He smiled.

"It's there. This is just a different kind."

"I like this version better," he told her, and helped her into the saddle. He retrieved the slender knife, cleaned it, and returned it to the calf holster.

Darkness came over the hills as he led the way north again and returned to the road that roughly paralleled the river.

"Who were they, Fargo?" Caroline asked.

"Drifters. Wahoos who couldn't resist what they thought were easy pickings," he said. "The country's full of them. No connection with those we're after."

She nodded with a sense of relief and rode through the new night beside him.

Caroline was growing up, Fargo reflected, the inside meeting the outside, whether she liked it or not. He kept a good pace as the moon rose, and the night had grown deep when the path returned to within sight of the river. A few dozen yards behind where he reined to a halt, the soft yellow glow of the *Shady Lady* moved through the darkness with deliberate slowness. He swung to the ground, undid his gun belt, and pulled off clothes down to his underdrawers, wrapped everything in his oilskin slicker, and saw Caroline slide to the ground before he stepped into the water.

She reached out one hand, pressed the palm against the skin of his smoothly muscled chest, much as a child might explore something new. She held her hand to him for a moment, slowly pulled it back. "See you tomorrow," she said.

"Ride along with the boat," he said.

"As much as the road lets me."

He turned from her, stepped from the shoreline, and lowered himself into the water, the oilskin wrapped around one arm. He swam out to meet the slowly moving boat and saw the gaming salon lights still blazed but most of the passenger cabins were dark. He reached the boat and clung with one hand to the edge of the main deck, which cleared the water by less than three feet. He let himself be pulled along while his eyes swept the deck. Satisfied that there were no crewmen near, he pulled himself aboard and moved to the stack of firewood in a crouch, undid the oilskin, and set his things out while he stretched out and let himself dry.

The boiler-room firewood stack was becoming a familiar hiding place, he reflected as he positioned himself where he had a clear view of the deck fore and aft. If he moved out to the gunwale, he could see the upper decks. Meanwhile, he could hear any sound from the center deck directly above him.

He settled back. He'd wait, let the night move to the new day, even if it turned out to be a waste of time. Waiting was made of wasted time. And on the morrow, he'd find a way to talk with Canyon. He relaxed and listened to the soft slap of the water against the sides of the boat.

8

The warm night air quickly dried him off. Fargo had just finished pulling on clothes when he glimpsed the figure moving along the deck outside the paddle-wheel housing. He straightened, watched the figure step from the deepest shadows, take on a slender shape, and become Darlene, still in her short-skirted working outfit with the small white apron. He stepped away from the wood as she made for the narrow steps to the second deck.

She halted as she saw him. "Fargo!" She frowned. "What are you doing here at this hour?"

"Just what I was going to ask you," he said, smiling.

She moved from the bottom step to face him. "Getting some air. I often take a walk around the boat when I finish work. It helps me relax and gets the cigar smoke out of my nose," she said, pausing to give him a sidelong glance. "I haven't seen you the last few days. I thought maybe you'd left us at St. Louis."

"No, I've been keeping to myself."

"That's too bad," she said with her warm smile. "Well, you know where my cabin is. The invitation still holds."

"That's nice to know," Fargo said as he caught the movement to his left and turned to see a figure come into view near the paddle wheel housing. A tall, broad-shouldered figure, the heavy face dour even in the dim light, Fargo saw Ez Crawley move toward him.

"When did you get back?" the man blurted, and Fargo saw Darlene's eyebrows go up.

"Keeping to yourself?" she slid at him.

"Didn't say it was on the boat," he said, and she gave a chiding glance. She turned away and went up the steps as Fargo faced Ez Crawley's frown.

"Captain Billy's been wondering and worrying," the man said. "Caroline with you?"

"She'll be along in the morning," Fargo said. "What brings you out here at this hour?"

"I always check the boilers and the paddle wheel. Do it every night when things are quiet," the man said, and turned to the steps. "I'll tell the captain you're here."

"Tell him I'll come visit when I'm ready," Fargo said.

"He'll want to talk to you now," Ez Crawley said with an edge in his voice.

"When I'm ready," Fargo said firmly, and Crawley turned and hurriedly climbed up the narrow stairs. Fargo watched him until he was out of sight and then returned to his place alongside the stacked wood. Darlene and Ez Crawley clambering about the boat in the dead of night, he reflected, his eyes narrowed. Had one of them been signaling to shore? Or meeting someone on board? Perhaps each other? He turned the questions in his mind. Both Darlene and Ez Crawley had perfectly reasonable answers for roaming the lower deck in the middle of the night. Just as they had for their trips ashore. But the best masks were reasonable ones, he reminded himself as he settled back against the wood. The night still had hours to go.

Canyon O'Grady sauntered from the gaming salon. There were only a few players left at Monica's table and he hadn't played well all night, losing for a rare instance. His mind had been cluttered, his concentration distracted with thoughts about what he'd learned in St. Louis and wondering why Fargo hadn't returned yet. Had he run into serious trouble? Canyon wondered as he strolled along the deck in the dark of the night. But Fargo was a man who could handle the unexpected, Canyon told himself. He halted at the low iron rail with its filigree design and scanned the dark river and the darker trees along the shore.

What he had learned in St. Louis continued to bother him. It didn't fit anywhere, not into Fargo's theories about the raids, not even into normal business procedures. But it was more than just not fitting, Canyon frowned. It added something unexplained and undefined, and he continued to have the feeling it was more than it seemed. A strange fact with a life of its own, he pondered as he stared into the river.

The sound of footsteps broke into his thoughts and he turned to see a man coming toward him, a face made of heavy folds.

"Got a match?" the man asked, and Canyon saw the cigarillo in his hand.

"Sorry, that's not one of my vices," O'Grady said.

The man halted, peered at him. "You're Fargo," he said.

Canyon smiled as instant caution rushed through him. "I might be," he said. "Why?"

"My friend behind you wants to meet you," the man said, and Canyon half-spun to see the second figure step from the shadows, a single-action Joslyn army revolver in his hand.

"Don't try anything," the man growled.

"What if I tell you I'm not Fargo?" Canyon asked.

The first man poked him in the back with the barrel of a gun. "We wouldn't much believe you," he growled. The man with the Joslyn had stepped closer, the gun leveled at his chest, Canyon saw. He felt the other gun pulled away from his back and heard the sudden movement behind him. He tried to duck away, but the butt of the gun smashed down on his head. He had but a moment to feel the sharp pain and then the gray curtain descended over him and he slumped to the deck.

Jake Brant pushed the gun into his waist and bent down to Canyon's unconscious form. "Now," he grunted. "Give a hand, dammit."

Sam Radar quickly bent over, took Canyon's legs and lifted along with Jake.

"He'll be just another body washed ashore downriver," Jake said. "If he ever surfaces. God knows how many bodies are held down in the Mississippi bottom mud."

Both men stepped back, swung their victim, and sent the body sailing over the rail and into the air. They peered down and watched the body hit the water with a heavy splash. "Now we stay low and get off at the first stop in the morning," Jake murmured in satisfaction.

"I can feel that bonus money in my pocket," Sam Radar chortled softly as both hurried down the deck.

*   *   *

Fargo pushed away from where he'd been sitting and bounded to his feet as he heard the loud, heavy splash. No bucket of water tossed overboard, not even a case of champagne, he murmured as he peered through the night. Straining his eyes, he scanned the river just beyond the stern of the boat. Then he halted, brought his eyes back again at a spot he'd passed, and saw the dark shape that had risen to the surface. "Goddamn," he hissed. Somebody had fallen from the upper deck, he muttered as he shed gun belt and clothes. He dived into the river, a powerful, long form spearing the air to enter the water with hardly a sound.

He came to the surface and found the dark shape now beyond the stern of the boat. He struck out with powerful strokes, the downriver current helping him to cut through the warm water. He reached the form just as it began to sink again, and he felt the shock course through him as he glimpsed the unruly red hair in the dim light of the moon.

"Shit," he bit out, almost leapt through the last few feet of water, and closed his arm around Canyon's shoulders. Keeping his head out of the water, Fargo pulled the limp form toward the shore as he swam with one arm while astonishment wrapped itself around him. He reached the shore and pulled Canyon onto the bank, turned him over onto his stomach. No blood, Fargo noted gratefully, no knife wound or bullet hole.

But Canyon O'Grady didn't go falling off boats, Fargo muttered. He frowned at Canyon's water-soaked form when he heard the groan, saw Canyon's head lift as he spit out a mouthful of the Mississippi, groan again, and rid himself of more water. He pushed himself up to a sitting position, turned, and stared at Fargo.

"By God, I never thought I'd see you as an angel but I am now," Canyon said.

"You're all right," Fargo said. "What the hell happened?"

O'Grady winced as he touched one finger to the back of his head. "Lucky for me I've such a thick head of hair," he muttered. "I'd have had a split skull otherwise. Worst of all, it was supposed to be for you."

"For me?"

"Two gents who were convinced I was you," Canyon said. "It all began in St. Louis and it'll take a bit of telling. I'd suggest we get back to the boat while we still have a chance."

"She's going upriver, and that's against the current," Fargo said as he rose to his feet. "We can catch her easily enough."

"We'll talk later," Canyon said. He pushed himself up and fell in beside Fargo, who set off in a steady trot along the riverbank.

The *Shady Lady*'s smokestacks were twin beacons of showery sparks that rose into the night. The strong downriver current held her to a snail's pace. It wasn't more than another fifteen minutes when the two figures ashore were trotting opposite the slow-moving craft. Fargo moved on for another two hundred yards before turning and plunging into the river. With Canyon swimming a few feet behind, he moved noiselessly through the warm water and reached the boat in midriver as it went by. He swung himself over the low gunwale and extended a helping hand to pull Canyon aboard.

Canyon rested for a moment on one knee and felt the dull, throbbing pain still in his head. "We can't talk in my cabin. Monica will come looking for me there."

"Caroline's cabin. She won't be back till morning," Fargo said, and led the way down the inside corridor of the boat, pausing every few feet to listen. But the corridor remained silent and empty. They reached Caroline's cabin, stepped inside, and turned the lamp on. Canyon shed wet clothes and Fargo found one of Caroline's towels and handed it to him and watched him first dry off the ivory-gripped Colt.

"I'm listening and damn curious," Fargo said.

"You first. What did you find out?" Canyon asked.

"I was right. Hired Indians, paid with wagonloads of whiskey," Fargo said. "But the damn grain disappeared. We thought they had it in the wagon, but they didn't."

"Sacks of grain don't disappear."

"You're sounding like Caroline. Only these sure as hell seemed to have. We retraced steps and came up empty."

Canyon frowned as he listened. "There's a lot in this that's not what it seems, I'm thinking," he said, and proceeded to recount what he had found in St. Louis. When he finished, Fargo's brow wore a deep crease.

"Damn strange, that's for sure," the Trailsman muttered.

"More than strange. Shipments don't arrive and the

haulage company doesn't file a claim, doesn't even send a wagon. Why not?" Canyon prodded. "Filing claims would be an important part of putting Captain Billy in a financial hole. It makes no sense unless . . ." He let the word trail off.

"Unless what?" Fargo asked.

"Unless you're all wrong about it. Maybe nobody's trying to put Captain Billy in a hole."

Fargo continued to frown. "Then why the raids? Why hire the Fox to make it look like nothing more than Indian raids? If it's not an attempt to put the captain in a hole, what is it?"

"I don't know," Canyon admitted. "I can't see all this just to steal some sacks of grain. That doesn't figure, either."

Fargo lowered himself at the edge of the bed. "Let's go over what we know. Shipments of grain are stolen. The Saux Fox are hired to make it look like nothing more than Indian raids. I've pinned that much down. The shipments are consigned to Fullerton Haulage in St. Louis. They never arrive, and not only doesn't Fullerton Haulage file no claims for missing shipments but they don't seem to give a damn."

"Only they *do* give a damn, lad," Canyon added. "They tried to kill me for nosing around, thinking I was you."

Fargo nodded with a grimace. "There's something else. I was told two of the first shipments reached St. Louis before the raids began. They were picked up, meaning Fullerton Haulage knew shipments were to arrive. Then why didn't they go to pick up the stolen shipments? Because they knew they weren't arriving?"

Canyon's lips pursed. "Could be that," he thought

aloud. "What if Fullerton Haulage was set up as a cover? That'd explain that warehouse that never stored anything."

"It would, but cover for what? You thinking they're part of whoever's trying to sink Captain Billy?" Fargo questioned.

"No," Canyon said. "They'd have filed claims for losses, then."

"Yes, dammit," Fargo agreed, bitterness in his voice. "So I've got a lot of unconnected facts that don't spell out anything and shoot holes in what I was thinking."

"Fullerton didn't come looking for the grain shipments. Didn't Captain Billy think that more than a little strange?" Canyon queried.

"I don't know. I never asked him. But I'm sure going to tomorrow."

"Don't forget about the two that tossed me overboard," Canyon said. "I'd guess they're still on board, and I'll be waiting for them when they try to leave."

"We'll be waiting for them," Fargo corrected, and O'Grady rose to his feet. "We've gone around in enough circles for now. Let's see what we can add tomorrow," Fargo said.

"I'm growing more and more sure of one thing: there's too much going on here to be a scheme to take an old man's boat. There's something more. I don't know what, but I'm going to sleep on it," Canyon said. "I'll be getting back to my cabin and wondering what I'm going to tell Monica about where I've been."

"Tell her you found that I was back on board and we've been talking," Fargo said.

Canyon considered the suggestion for a moment. "That's as good as anything. She knows I'd want to tell you what I found in St. Louis, so it's only a half-lie," he said. "She's not happy about my helping you."

"Maybe she isn't, but I am. I appreciate it, old friend," Fargo said. "Nothing at your end of things yet?"

"Nothing. Helping you keeps me from being completely frustrated," Canyon said, and paused at the door to look back. "I owe you another, lad."

"I'm not counting." Fargo laughed and Canyon hurried down the corridor. Fargo let him disappear before he stepped outside and made his way to the wood stack where he'd shed his gun belt. He reached the place and had just strapped the gun belt on when a tall, slender shape stepped from the deep shadows beside the paddle-wheel housing.

"Fargo," Monica said, surprise in her voice.

"In person." He smiled. "What are you doing out here at this hour?"

"Canyon's disappeared. I'm scouring the boat for him," she said, concern in her voice.

"He's in his cabin."

"No. I've been there twice."

"Try for three," Fargo said. "We've been together. He's been telling me about what he found out at St. Louis."

"Damn him, he didn't have to just disappear," Monica snapped with more than annoyance.

"He had a lot to tell me," Fargo said placatingly, but Monica's lovely lips stayed thin.

"Yes, I know," she said. "Did you get the answers you wanted chasing after those Indians?"

"I thought I did. Now I'm not sure," Fargo said honestly.

"That's too bad," she said with more politeness than feeling, then she turned on her heel and hurried up the steps.

Canyon would need to use all his charm, Fargo reckoned. A voice broke off his idle thoughts and he turned to see a short, round-faced figure coming along the deck.

"Fargo! I've been looking all over for you," Captain Billy said, and Fargo saw the man's usually pleasant face so drawn that it seemed to lose its roundness. "I turned the wheel over to Ez as soon as he told me you were aboard. What happened? Where's Caroline?"

"She'll be boarding at Keokuk," Fargo said. When he finished telling Billy everything, the captain frowned into the night for a long moment.

"I sure can't make any sense out of it, if that's what you're expecting," Captain Billy grumbled. "What's Canyon O'Grady doing in it?"

"Just trying to help me out," Fargo said. "But you can tell me about Fullerton Haulage."

"What would I know about them?" Billy returned.

"Didn't you think it damn strange that they never came looking for the grain shipments that had been raided? Not the last one and not the others, yet they did pick up the first two shipments that came through."

"Not really. The truth is that many of these haulage outfits keep such poor records that half the time they don't know what they're supposed to pick up. When we still have cargo on board an hour before sailing, we send a man out to the shipping outfit and tell them to come pick up their stuff. It happens all the time."

"So you figured Fullerton Haulage was just more of the same," Fargo said.

146

"That's right. I sure wasn't going to go tell them their shipments had been raided. Didn't see any good in that for me."

"Naturally."

"I decided to lay back and wait for as long as I could. Truth is, I didn't have much choice," Captain Billy said ruefully, and Fargo nodded. The explanation had been simple and perfectly understandable. Fargo wondered why it failed to satisfy him. "What next?" Captain Billy asked.

"I've a few more things to explore," Fargo said.

"I'd like you not to take Caroline out chasing leads. It's too dangerous."

"Caroline's a strong-minded young woman. You tell her."

"I damn sure will," the captain said. "It's all getting to me, Fargo. It's like waiting for an ax to fall on your neck. I'm thinking that if I lose another shipment, I might just pack it in before it all comes down on me."

"What good will that do you?" Fargo demanded.

"No good, but I'd rather walk away then be forced away," the captain said.

"Give me a little more time before you do that," Fargo said.

Captain Billy's shrug was made of resignation as he trudged up the stairway to the wheelhouse.

Fargo returned to Caroline's cabin, stretched out on the bed, and let thoughts revolve inside him. But exhaustion was a demand that refused to be pushed aside, and he shut off thoughts and let sleep rush over him. He fell into the deep sleep of fatigue and stayed wrapped in it until the abrupt change in the motion of the boat woke him. He saw daylight through the cabin window. He sat up, swung from the bed, and peered through the window to see the dockside and the long, flat buildings behind.

"Damn," he swore, strapped on his gun belt, and ran from the cabin onto the deck. He glanced up to see Canyon, flame hair still tousled from sleep, rush out on the upper deck as he struggled into his shirt.

The gangplank had already been lowered and Fargo was first to reach the crewman standing beside the bollard. "Anybody leave the ship yet?" he asked as Canyon came on the run.

"Two gents. We hardly had the gangplank down," the crewman said.

"On foot?" Fargo asked, Canyon at his shoulder.

"Yes." The crewman nodded.

Fargo turned to meet Canyon's grim-lipped glance. "It'll be a damn long walk back to St. Louis," Canyon said. "They'll be getting horses. I'll get Cormac."

"Wait," Fargo said as his gaze fastened on the cluster of figures staring at the paddle wheel at the stern of the boat. Captain Billy, Ez Crawley, and two crewmen, he noted as he walked toward the small knot of muttering figures. "Something wrong?" he asked as Canyon followed him.

"Sure as hell is," Captain Billy snapped. "Look at that, will you? One of the paddle wheels is hanging loose. Sprung its shaft. I could feel something wrong for a few hours before we docked."

"How would that happen?" Fargo asked.

"Sometimes a hub loosens, falls off, and the paddle slips the shaft. But usually it's a damn branch that comes up, catches in the paddle, and jams it. The paddle twists, the eccentric strap snaps, the hub goes, and the paddle comes off the shaft. It means we'll be here all day for repairs. I've got to send Ez all the way to Burlington to get a new hub."

Fargo kept his voice casual. "Would the same thing happen if a piece of wood fell into the paddle wheel?" he inquired.

"Sure. It'd act just the same way a thick branch from underneath would," the captain said. "Why?"

"Nothing, really. Just that I noticed some loose pieces of firewood on the deck. I wondered if one of them might have fallen in," Fargo said, turned away, and Canyon fell in step beside him.

"If a piece of wood fell in," O'Grady murmured. "Very diplomatic. What you mean is if a piece of wood were tossed in."

Fargo smiled. "It's a very convenient accident. Now anyone on board has the whole day to make a contact ashore."

"Yes, but meanwhile, we've two gents to make contact with," Canyon said, and hurried to the stable at the rear of the boat.

Fargo glanced up and saw Caroline moving along the dockside on the gelding, the Ovaro in tow. He raced toward her and swung onto the Ovaro without slowing his stride.

"What's going on?" Caroline frowned as she tossed him the reins.

"We'll talk later. I've things to tell you," he said, wheeled the horse around as Canyon came out on the magnificent palomino and fell into a fast canter alongside him. "Dammit, this is what comes from not getting enough sleep," Fargo said. "I should've been up before dawn."

"It also comes from staying up all night trying to soothe ruffled feathers," Canyon said. "I'd guess those two dry-gulchers have already bought themselves horses."

"So we first find a horse dealer," Fargo said, and his gaze swept the flat-roofed buildings that stretched in a half-wheel arc beyond the dockside. Keokuk was one of those towns that really had no life of their own. Like land-based barnacles, they clung to the shores of the Mississippi and lived on the traffic and energy spawned by the great river. He glimpsed a saloon, a general store, three warehouses, and a blacksmith as they rode. The spread-out houses fell behind as they rode on and he heard Canyon call to him.

"Over there," Canyon said.

Fargo looked to his right to see the fences of a two-corral spread, a half-dozen horses in each corral and a small house alongside. He reached the house a few paces behind Canyon and saw the weathered sign over the door: MURPHY—HORSES FOR SALE.

A man in too-large overalls stepped from the house and his practiced eye immediately went from the gleaming Ovaro to the palomino and back again. "You boys sure don't look like you need horses," he observed dryly.

"Very astute," Canyon said. "You have any customers this morning?"

"Two fellers," the man said. "Bought two of my oldest and cheapest plugs."

Fargo exchanged glances with Canyon. "Just enough to get them back to St. Louis," Canyon said.

Fargo wheeled the Ovaro around. "Let's try along the riverbank first," he said, and led the way to the shore, where he turned south and let the pinto move with his feet in the soft, cool mud of the bank. He rode with his eyes sweeping the ground and reined to a halt before they'd gone a quarter-mile. "No tracks," he grunted. "They didn't go this way."

"Damn," Canyon breathed. "There could be fifty ways they could've gone inland."

"They'll stay near the river. It's the most direct route," Fargo said, and his eyes spotted a length of land that rose along a straight line southward. Not tall enough to call high land, but it would have to do, he muttered silently, and sent the Ovaro streaking toward the row of cockspar haw that covered the ridge. He turned south on the ridge and let his eyes sweep the land to his left. "They'll be down there somewhere, taking one of the deer trails whenever they can," he said. "And with the horses they have they'll be moving slow. We'll catch them soon enough."

"You really think somebody tossed a log into that paddle wheel, Fargo?" Canyon asked.

"I've been chasing down Indians. You've been nosing around. Somebody's getting nervous. I think plans need to be checked out again," Fargo said.

"Somebody. You still figure it's a scheme to get Captain Billy?" Canyon asked.

"I don't know what I think now, except one thing: you were right last night. This is more than it seems," Fargo said, and broke off conversation. "We'll talk more later." He gestured to the two riders in the distance below.

Canyon rode at his side as the Trailsman started to send the Ovaro down the slope.

"Wait," Canyon said. "I'll go on ahead and come down in front of them. You come up behind."

"Good idea," Fargo said, and let the palomino get a start across the low ridge. He waited till the pale-bronze horse was almost out of sight before spurring the pinto into a gallop. He reached the low terrain, turned south, and kept the horse at a gallop. He saw the two figures ahead grow larger.

Fargo was within a few dozen feet of the two men when they heard him and turned in the saddle to peer back, hands on their guns. He slowed. They kept their gaze on him as he moved toward them at a slow trot. He saw their hands half-draw six-guns out of holsters.

Canyon's voice cut through the air, and the two men spun on their horses to stare forward.

"You lads believe in ghosts?" Canyon asked mildly. Fargo rode up and saw the two men stare at the big flame-haired figure in front of them, both their jaws hanging open. "You see, you threw the wrong fellow overboard and that doesn't count. So I'm back," Canyon said.

Jake Brant found his voice first. "Goddamn, kill him," he croaked.

"Don't try it," Fargo barked, and saw the man's hand freeze on his gun. Jake Brant turned to look back at him and dropped his hand to his side. "That's smart," Fargo said, and saw the other man with hands half-raised in the air. He moved forward, reached over, took the six-gun from Jake Brant's holster, emptied it, and tossed it away. He glanced forward and saw Canyon do the same with the other man. "Now, you two answer some questions and you can walk away alive," Fargo said, and saw the two men exchange glances.

"We'll talk if you take us to St. Louis first," Jake

Brant said, and Fargo glanced at Canyon as the big red-haired man brought the palomino around to come alongside him.

"Why?" Fargo asked. "So your friends can save you there?"

"You must take us for fools," Canyon said. "What's Fullerton Haulage?"

"A haulage outfit," Sam Radar said. "That's all we know."

"You can do better than that. I'm a man of little patience," Canyon said. "And my friend, here, has even less."

"We're hired help. We don't know anything," Jake Brant said.

Canyon drew the ivory-gripped Colt and saw Sam Radar's eyes widen. "We only need one of you to talk," O'Grady said.

"How do we know you'll let us go if we talk?" Sam Radar said.

"You'll have to take our word on it," Canyon snapped.

"If we talk, they'll know and we're dead," Jake Brant muttered. "They'll know. We talk and we have to move fast. We'll need our own horses. Get us to St. Louis and we'll talk."

"Forget it," Fargo growled.

"Take us halfway there," Jake Brant said. "Halfway there and we'll talk. Give us a chance to save our necks."

Canyon exchanged glances with Fargo. "Halfway there," he repeated, and shrugged. "What have we got to lose?"

"I don't know, but I don't like it. They're stalling," Fargo said.

"We take them halfway," Canyon said, well aware that both men heard everything said. "They don't talk, they're dead."

"We'll give it a try," Fargo said, and spoke to Jake Brant. "You two ride in front of us. One wrong move and you know what happens."

The two men sent their horses forward and Canyon rode alongside Fargo some half-dozen yards behind. "Maybe they really are afraid of something," Canyon muttered in a voice only Fargo could hear. "Maybe they'll need to cut out fast."

"They're stalling. I just don't know why yet," Fargo whispered back.

Canyon shrugged and fell silent and they rode for a little over an hour more when Jake Brant drew to a halt.

"This horse is wheezin' real bad. He's got to rest a spell," the man said.

Fargo nodded and watched the man dismount. The other thick-chested man swung to the ground also. A double-row of thick brush ran alongside where the two men had dismounted. Staying in the saddle, Fargo watched Jake Brant mop his brow with a stained kerchief and put his head down to the horse's jugular groove to listen to the animal's breathing. He stayed there for a moment, straightened, and started to turn away.

Fargo caught the faint movement of his arm. Jake was reaching inside his shirt. Fargo's hand flew to the Colt at his side. He had the big Colt out of the holster as Jake Brant spun. Fargo saw the pepperbox, self-cocking pistol in his hand. He ducked to his left as Brant fired and felt the first two blasts of the revolving barrels go past his head. He fired the Colt as the man got off another two barrels and Jake Brant staggered back, dropped the small pistol, and collapsed on the ground, a red stain instantly seeping out from his shirt.

Sam Radar had raced into the thick brush and Fargo saw Canyon going after him on the palomino. The single shot echoed a few seconds later and Fargo cursed inwardly as he slid from the saddle and watched Canyon reappear out of the brush.

"He had a knife on him. Came at me with it," Canyon said.

Fargo picked up the pepperbox pistol and looked at it. "Blunt and Symes, six barrels," he grunted, and tossed the weapon atop Jake Brant's lifeless form. "That's why they were stalling. We had them front and back. They didn't dare try anything then, so they stalled for time," he said.

"Dedication?" Canyon wondered aloud.

"Damn fools, more likely," Fargo said, and pulled himself back onto the pinto. "But they won't be giving us any answers. Except what they already have."

"Meaning what?" Canyon frowned.

"They tried to kill you just for getting too close to something. You said it last night. It's too much, too heavy just to be about getting an old man's boat. Too many turns and twists," Fargo said, and told him what Captain Billy had said regarding haulage outfits in general and his handling of Fullerton.

"That explains his actions reasonably enough," Canyon said.

"Only we know now that Fullerton Haulage is more than some inefficient little haulage outfit," Fargo said. "If someone set up raids to steal grain shipments to put the captain in a hole, why not just do it? Why set up a phony warehouse operation and a haulage outfit? There has to be a lot more to it."

"Such as?"

Fargo let a grim smile touch his lips as he kept the pinto at a walk beside Canyon. "I remember you said that first night I came aboard that two sets of rascals had brought us together at the same spot. I'm thinking maybe they're not two sets of rascals," he said.

"Go on," Canyon said.

"Washington expects the gold to be shipped downriver on the *Shady Lady,* into St. Louis, right?"

"Right. Missouri being a state that southern forces can operate in freely." Canyon nodded.

"But you've seen no signs of any shipments."

"Right again."

"And no agent on board."

"That's not unusual. A good agent could be damn hard to spot," Canyon said.

"But no grain shipments reached St. Louis, either, except the first two," Fargo pressed. "No grain shipments and no gold shipments."

Canyon stared back as he let the substance of Fargo's words sink in. "Because they're one and the same thing," he murmured finally. "By God, it might just be."

"It's the only way it all fits. Fullerton Haulage and the warehouse were set up as a cover to receive smuggled gold shipments, not sacks of grain. That's the only way it makes sense. And it'd also explain why they didn't come to pick up the grain when it had been raided."

"Why?"

"There had to be some kind of signal from the boat to the shore before she docked at St. Louis," Fargo said. "I'm sure the gold shipments weren't on a timetable. They expected some would be delayed. No signal, no shipment aboard, and no need to pick up."

"By God, it does all fit. It does make sense, except for one thing. Let's go along with your thinking. They're smuggling the gold in as sacks of grain. They've set up this elaborate fake-warehouse-and-haulage-outfit cover to receive it. They have everything in place and working. Why hire the Fox to steal the sacks of grain? That doesn't fit in at all."

Fargo grimaced. "I know it doesn't, dammit, and I haven't come up with an answer for that. Not yet, anyway. But the rest of it fits. I say we go with the rest of it for now."

Canyon shrugged. "I haven't anything better."

"It even fits what happened last night, wrecking the paddle wheel," Fargo said. "I'm thinking that something isn't right at their end and they had to arrange a meeting to go over things."

"With the agent on board. It does fit," Canyon said. "Dammit, who the hell do they have on the boat?"

"My personal guess is Ez Crawley, but it could be anybody, including little Darlene. She was near the paddle wheel last night. Getting air, she said. Any of the crew would've been able to jam the paddle, also."

"Let's get back and find out who went ashore. Maybe that'll tell us something," Canyon said.

"It won't," Fargo said, and drew a frown. "On a whole day's stopover, everybody will go ashore. You said it yourself, no mistakes, no wrong moves. Somebody is clever and careful."

"Maybe this time they had to leave themselves open,"

Canyon said. "Hell, there's nothing much to do in Keokuk. Whoever we want had to go farther. Maybe we can find out who went off on their own for a long time."

Fargo's laugh was grim. "Sorry to throw water on you, friend, but I'll bet a lot of folks aboard went off all day. Fort Madison's just up a ways. They could rent a wagon and go shopping at the Indian trading posts outside the fort. There are a lot of them. Crew members not needed could just go off into the trees and relax. And you heard Captain Billy say he'd have to send Ez Crawley all the way to Burlington for a hub."

"Logic can be a burden as well as a blessing. Let's ride," Canyon growled.

9

"What the hell are you talking about?" the man bit out, his bushy brows knitted together.

"I'm talking about your being clever."

"Clever?"

"Yes. I presume you sent for me to tell me about it."

"Clever about what, dammit?"

"The Indian raids."

"I contacted you to tell me why there've been no goddamn shipments, and you want to know about my being clever?"

"Didn't you stage the Indian raids on the shipments?"

"I didn't stage any raids anywhere. I don't know what you're talking about."

"Every shipment except the first two has been raided by the Saux Fox and carried off. Are you telling me that wasn't your doing?"

"You're damn right I am. I don't know anything about any Indian raids. Why the hell would I set up Indian raids on the shipments?"

"I assumed you'd found out something or other and had to come up with a change of plans in a hurry. I was thinking you'd learned that Washington had come onto the St. Louis operation, so you staged the raids to get everything off before we docked at St. Louis."

"No, dammit, nothing of the kind. I didn't stage any raids."

"My God, you weren't being clever?"

"No. Are you telling me our gold has been carried off in a bunch of goddamn Indian raids?"

"Yes, that's exactly what's been going on. Only I thought you were behind it. I was giving you credit for being quick and clever. I see I was wrong."

"Don't go being smart-ass with me. How the hell was I supposed to know what was going on? All I knew was that we kept looking for a signal and shipments, and we never got either. I told the others something was wrong. They kept not believing me."

"Something is very much wrong."

"Good God, this is a disaster. What can you tell me about those goddamn raids? You were on board."

"Not a hell of a lot. The Saux Fox raided the boat and made off with all the sacks in every shipment."

"That bastard Fargo still on board?"

"He is."

"He been a problem?"

"I didn't think so. I do now."

"What's that mean?"

"He's been trying to catch the Fox and get the grain sacks back. He chased after them the last time around."

"Did he get the sacks back?"

"No."

"Then where the hell are the grains sacks with our gold?"

"I haven't any idea. Fargo's convinced the raids were staged to make them look like nothing more than Indian raids. He really thinks somebody wants to stick the captain with a loss he can't meet and take over the boat."

The bushy-browed man glowered. "Goddamn, he might just be right."

"Are you serious?"

"You're damn right I'm serious. You thought I'd staged the raids. Now you know it wasn't me, and no damn Indians are going to raid a riverboat for grain sacks. Somebody trying to get at the captain has near a million dollars of our gold and doesn't know it."

"I suppose that is possible."

"It's more than possible. It's exactly what's been happening, don't you see? God Almighty, we've got to find out who it is, where the grain is, and get it back before somebody else does."

"Fargo said it just disappeared on him."

"The hell with Fargo. Let him keep on thinking he's chasing grain sacks. I'll find them."

"How?"

"I've a standby force up here, sent up about a month ago in case I'd need them. I'll get them to scour the whole damn territory and more. Whoever took the grain has to be around here someplace."

"Scouring the countryside will be like looking for a needle in a haystack. We need something better than that."

"You got any ideas?"

"You get your standby force together. I expect another shipment will be put aboard at Winona, just as all the others were. You know the drop there?"

"I know it."

161

"I'll have a plan and instructions for you there."

"Whatever you say. You're the agent in charge. All I know is that this is one hell of a kettle of fish. We set everything up to get the gold through under the nose of Washington's people and now some goddamn small-time fool blows it sky-high."

"It's not hopeless. If Washington has an agent on board, he doesn't know anything about anything, and Fargo still thinks he's chasing sacks of grain. We're the only ones that know what's really been happening. We'll salvage it."

"You, not me. You made the assumptions."

"So I did. My mistake. I should've realized you couldn't be that clever. Just get your standby force together."

The bushy-browed man glowered and strode away.

The afternoon neared an end when Fargo and Canyon reached Keokuk. While Canyon stabled the horses, Fargo stepped to where Captain Billy waited on the deck, concern in his round face.

"I was getting worried about you. We'll be sailing in fifteen minutes," Billy said.

"Got everything fixed, I take it," Fargo said.

"We got the paddle straightened while Ez was getting the new hub in Burlington. He just got back with it a few minutes ago," Captain Billy said. "You and O'Grady come onto anything?"

"Not really. But I can tell you this much: I think maybe there's more going on here than either you or I suspected," Fargo said, and drew a look of immediate interest from Captain Billy.

"Like what?" the man queried.

"I'm not ready to say yet, but I'm working on it."

"I'll be damn interested," Billy said.

Fargo watched some of the passengers returning to the boat and saw Darlene come past him with one of the crewmen in tow. "You have a nice time ashore?" Fargo asked casually.

"I did. Enjoyed every minute of it," she said with an edge of tartness.

"Sort of an unexpected day off." Fargo smiled.

"Exactly," she said.

"What'd you do?" he asked, still keeping his voice casual.

"Roamed around by myself for a while and then Ned, here, met up with me," she said, and wriggled her rear as she went on.

Two older couples came past and nodded.

"Have a nice day?" Fargo smiled.

"Oh, yes, we hired a surrey and drove to the Indian trading posts outside Fort Madison. A lot of the passengers did," one of the women said. "It was amusing."

"I'll bet it was." Fargo smiled and the foursome moved on. He went down the deck to meet Canyon as Captain Billy began to climb to the wheelhouse. "As I expected, everybody was off someplace," he muttered. "Caroline will be full of questions. How much should I tell her?"

"Tell her about the gold and you'll have to tell her how you found out about it. I don't want that yet," Canyon said.

"I'll tell her that I thought the two men we went after knew about the grain, but that I was wrong," Fargo said. "What are you telling Monica?"

"Pretty much the same thing," Canyon answered. "You thought you were onto something and I tagged along. She can't get much madder at me than she is now."

"I feel like I'm responsible for breaking up something good," Fargo said.

"I'll put it back together when this is over," Canyon said brightly.

"That's called having confidence in your own charms."

"The result of past victories, lad." Canyon laughed and hurried away.

Fargo turned and began the walk to Caroline's cabin as he felt the boat get under way and heard the big paddle wheels splash noisily in the shallow water. He reached the cabin as night descended. He knocked and Caroline opened, her round face grave.

"Good, I've been waiting for you," she murmured, and he saw she was clad in a floor-length, cotton nightgown with a square neck that showed the rise of her round breasts. "I just woke an hour ago," she said, and he stepped into the cabin and sat down on the edge of the bed. She was as full of eager questions as he had expected and he satisfied her curiosity with half-truths, finishing with a last answer that was close enough to the truth.

"We have to find those sacks of grain. That's probably the most important thing now. Then we can find who's behind it," he said. "That's why Canyon went with me after those two men this morning."

"He certainly has been awfully nice about helping you," Caroline said, and he shot a quick glance at her and decided she wasn't probing.

"He's that kind," Fargo said.

"You going to stay up all night again on deck?"

"No need to until there's another shipment on board," Fargo said. "I'm going to rest, relax, and think some more."

Caroline turned and a round little rear pressed into the nightgown for an instant. She went to one of the dresser drawers and returned with a bottle of bourbon and two small glasses. "This will help you relax," she said, poured a glass for him and half as much for herself.

"Bourbon in the dresser? Is this a hidden vice?"

"No hidden vice. Captain Billy always told me to keep a bottle of bourbon on hand for colds and aches. To find the grain," she said, and raised her glass.

"I'll sure drink to that," Fargo said, and answered the toast with his own glass. The bourbon was smooth and he let himself enjoy the warm richness of it. "Maybe there's an extra cabin I can use this trip," Fargo said as he sipped the whiskey.

"There's always Darlene," Caroline sniffed.

"She seems to have one of the crewmen on the line," Fargo said.

"You can stay here," Caroline said softly, staring into his glass as she sat down beside him.

"Thanks, but I'd like a bed instead of the floor tonight."

"You can have the bed," she murmured, still not looking up from the glass.

"Where will you go?"

"No place," she said, and this time looked up, her brown eyes deep. He felt her arms lift, go around his neck, and then her lips were on his, sweet, gentle eagerness, until she finally pulled back. "When you left last night, I almost called to you to come back," she said. "I suddenly didn't want you to leave me. I suddenly realized a lot of things about what I wanted." Her mouth found his again, pressing, tentative yet eager. This time he pulled back and saw the nightgown had slipped over one lovely, round, smooth shoulder.

He reached out and brought the nightgown up to cover her shoulder as he frowned at her. "You expecting me to make love to you?" he asked with shock in his voice. "Why, I can't do that, honey. Sleeping with someone you held on your knee only eight years ago is wrong. I was told that, and I'm not one to be told something twice."

"Damn you, Fargo," Caroline hissed.

He drained the bourbon, put the glass on the dresser, and rose to his feet, pausing to look back at her. She had let both straps of the nightgown fall and the top of the garment rested precariously on the high breasts. Her eyes held his, round and dark.

"You telling me to forget what I was told?" he asked. Caroline drew her breath in. The high breasts moved and the top of the nightgown fell to her waist. "I do believe you are," Fargo murmured as he took in the very round white breasts, each tipped by a pale-pink point and an equally pale-pink small circle. An almost small barrel-chested set of ribs was visible beneath her breasts.

Caroline stood up and let the rest of the nightgown slip from her to land at her ankles. Fargo saw the vibrancy in her compact figure at once—slightly convex little belly, a deep dense triangle, and legs that were plainly strong yet with a nice curve to them.

He shed his gun belt, pulled his shirt off, and stepped to her. Her arms lifted, circled his neck, and she fell back onto the bed with him. His hand circled one breast and caressed its firm softness, her skin silken smooth. A little gasp came from her as his thumb moved back and forth across the pale-pink tip. He brought his mouth to hers, pressed, pushed harder, and her lips opened. He let his tongue search her mouth and felt her fingers tighten against the back of his neck. His lips traced a simmering path along her neck, down to one round breast, and closed upon the tiny pale-pink tip.

"Ah, ah . . . oooooh," Caroline gasped out as he let his tongue circle the tiny tip, dance upon the top of the little nipple. He felt it lift and grow fuller as Caroline cried out in pleasure. He drew in more of the breast until it filled his mouth and he pulled gently. Caroline's hands left his neck to dig into his back and he heard low, gasped sounds from her. His hand danced slowly along the compact body, across the round, full ribs, pressed into the little mound of her belly, and then pushed deep into the dense black triangle. He pressed gently, stroked, pressed again, and felt the fleshy Venus mound rise, offer itself, a hirsute messenger. His hand slid lower, where her soft skin had grown damp.

"Oh, no . . . oh, no . . . no . . ." Caroline murmured even as he felt the skin between her thighs grow damper, her thighs fall open for an instant and come together again. But his hand slid down in that instant and cupped around the dark and hidden places.

Caroline's torso arched, the firm breasts pushing

167

upward as a long, crying half-scream came from her. His hand pressed and touched, felt moist, luscious softness. Again Caroline cried out, a scream of panic and pleasure, fear and frenzy. He paused, waited, let his mouth pull in a breast and caressed it gently with his tongue. "Ah, aaaaah, aaaah," Caroline breathed, and he felt her body relax in pleasure.

He continued to gently caress her breast as he moved his hand again and touched the wet warmth once more. This time her cry held a new wanting in it. He explored, made contact with the voluptuous softness of her, stroked gently, and Caroline's hips surged upward, twisted, fell back again. The damp skin of her inner thighs clamped against his arm and her legs rubbed against him with an entreaty of their own. "Oh God, oh . . . oh, God yes," Caroline breathed, words hardly audible, but words weren't needed as her flesh spoke. Her body called out and he brought his own throbbing firmness atop her, touched against the dense bush. Her firm, compact legs fell open, her torso lifted. He slid forward and felt the wild wetness engulf him, sweet hot walls embracing. Caroline cried out again, her voice taking on new strength. He slid deeper, drew back, thrust again, and her legs were around him, her thighs moist grips of a sweet vise. She cried out with his every motion.

"Yes, yes, yes, oh, God, oh yes . . . iiiieeee," Caroline gasped, pushed back, moved with him. She became one with him and her very being entwined with his, her flesh becoming his, his passion hers. He felt a touch of surprise at the hunger of her, the almost harsh way she swept aside new pains, new fears, new tensions. Caroline was a natural talent, he realized, her firm compact body fashioned to burst out of itself with wanting, the senses allowing no interference from the mind. He plunged into the consummate wildness with her. Suddenly her hands pulled his face to her breasts and held him there. He felt her hips quiver, rise, stay to tremble in midair. "Now, now, oh, migod now . . . aaaaiiii," Caroline screamed. He let himself explode with her, the world erupting in a shower of exquisite ecstasy.

She stayed suspended, held against him, gasped small breaths, and quivered until the timeless moment shattered and the world ceased its whirling. He heard the deep cry of despair as she sank down on the bed. He stayed with her.

"Oh, my," Caroline gasped finally, keeping her thighs around him, wanting him with her, unwilling to let the flesh grow separate. But with another sigh she let her legs slide down to stretch out alongside his muscled thighs, and he turned to lie beside her. His gaze moved up and down the firm, compact body and enjoyed the beauty of it, the glorious loveliness of the round breasts and the youthful firmness of her. Her body seemed to radiate energy even at rest.

"You're a surprise, Caroline," he said.

"To myself as much as to you," she murmured, and turned to press herself against him. Her lips fluttered softly into his chest and the firm breasts were sweet pillows against him. "It was much better," she murmured.

"Better?"

A smug smile edged her lips. "Better than being bounced on your knee," she said.

He laughed. "I do believe you've grown up, girl," he said, and she nodded. She pressed herself hard into him and in minutes he heard the steady sound of her in sleep.

Fargo lay on his back with one arm around her and thoughts slid back into his mind like so many thieves in the night, unwilling to let him just fall asleep in comfort. He let thoughts idle, tumble freely through his mind in loose association, and he reached over and turned out the lamp to plunge the cabin into blackness. But the other darkness seemed only to make inner thoughts more vivid, and he resigned himself to letting everything that had happened parade through his mind, pause, turn for examination, and drift on.

Caroline had been hard asleep in his arms for more than an hour when he almost sat up, his eyes snapping open. He let the thoughts dance in his mind. A smile came to his lips and he forced himself not to utter a small cry of triumph. It had blazed into clarity all of itself, facts sorting themselves out, the half-asleep mind seeing in ways the fully conscious one didn't. He'd had it happen before and each time he had to wonder at the workings of the mind. But the answer had been there all the time, and the smile still on his lips, he pulled Caroline to him and heard her murmur as he finally let himself fall asleep.

"You still sulking?" Canyon asked the willowy, onyx-haired form on the edge of the cabin bed, her beautifully curved, pale-white breasts hardly contained by the filmy black negligee.

"I don't sulk," Monica said.

"You're awfully quiet tonight," Canyon said.

"Perhaps so."

"Seems as though you're thinking hard about something."

Monica didn't reply for a long minute and then turned blue eyes on him that were edged with frost in a long stare. "Are you and that Fargo the only ones allowed to think?" she said with disdain.

"No, not at all," Canyon said. "Why'd you stop by wearing that next-to-nothing frill if all you're going to do is sit around and think?"

"Maybe just to let you see what you'll be missing if you keep on helping Fargo," she said icily.

"Torment is always sharper than words, I concede," Canyon said. "It's just that he saved my life, you know that, and he needs the help. This whole thing may be getting out of hand."

"Meaning what?"

Canyon picked words with care, shifting the thrust of them to Fargo. "He thinks this may be a lot bigger than he first thought."

"How?" Monica asked, frowning.

"He still thinks somebody's trying to do in Captain Billy, but he thinks there's more to it than that," Canyon said.

Monica tossed back a half-incredulous glance. "Now why would he suddenly think that?"

"He hasn't really told me yet." Canyon shrugged.

"Has he told you anything, really, or is he just using you?" Monica asked as she turned and let her arms come around his neck.

"He's not using me," Canyon said. "He's not that kind."

"I don't want anything to happen to you, Canyon. I've plans for us, I told you that," she said. "I never expected to meet anyone like you at this job. But now that I have, I don't want to lose you."

"A gambling man has to travel on," Canyon said, not ungently.

"Are you trying to turn me away?"

"No, I'm saying that plans can be difficult to make for some people," Canyon said.

"I'm not afraid. I'm good at convincing," Monica said, and the frilly negligee fell away as she proceeded to prove her words.

10

Fargo had already slipped from the bed, washed, and dressed in the light of the new morning when Caroline stirred and woke. She sat up and rubbed sleep from her eyes, her breasts deliciously beautiful as a sliver of sunlight came through the cabin window to touch the tiny pale-pink tips.

"Where are you going?" she asked.

"To look around, talk to Canyon, put our heads together," he said. "You going to be working on the books today?"

"Yes," she said. "But it'll be hard for me to concentrate. I know I'll keep thinking about the grain sacks and where they might be."

"Leave that to me," Fargo said. "You think about anyone who had an argument with Captain Billy, anybody who might want to see him go under."

"I have thought about that, ever since you told me you thought that was behind it. I haven't come up with anyone."

"Keep thinking. And I'll ask Billy. He might have an idea."

"Wait," she cried out as he turned to go. He stepped

to the bed. She clung to him instantly, all warm soft-ness that made the night flash in his mind. "I'm al-ready waiting for tonight," she whispered.

"Don't set your thoughts too hard, honey," he said more gruffly than he'd intended, and drew a moment's hurt from her eyes. "I meant something might get in the way," he said, and she let the hurt slip from her face.

"If it doesn't?" she asked.

"I'll be here," he said, and she allowed a slightly smug smile to touch her lips.

He hurried from the cabin and stepped onto the outer deck, leaned on the low wrought-iron rail, and waited. It wasn't a long wait before Canyon appeared on the deck above and climbed down to him. "Your charm work last night?" Fargo asked.

"Her caring did," Canyon said. "I tried pulling back some. Didn't have much success at that."

"Trying to toss her a cushion for when you have to tell her the truth about Canyon O'Grady?"

"More or less. She cares. She can care too much," Canyon said.

"Getting hurt is part of caring, I guess. Maybe it ought not be that way, but it always seems to come to that." He paused, moved closer to Canyon, and dropped his voice to barely more than a whisper, but the ex-citement was still in it. "I've something more impor-tant than Monica, delicious as she is," he said. "I've the answer to the last piece that wouldn't fit."

"I want to hear this," Canyon muttered.

"It came to me last night, but it was there all the time. We were so put off by what didn't make any sense that we couldn't see the answer right in front of us. They're smuggling the gold in the grain sacks.

They have everything set up to bring the gold through. They've an agent aboard to signal when a shipment is ready to pick up. With all that, they wouldn't steal their own shipments. We were right about all of that. It makes no sense."

"So what does make sense?"

"Somebody else staged the raids and stole the grain. Somebody out to put Captain Billy behind the eight ball. I was right all along about that part of it," Fargo said excitedly.

Canyon stared for a moment and then uttered a harsh sound. "Jesus, Joseph, and Mary! Of course, that has to be it," he said. "You were right about that part of it." He paused and his lips drew back in distaste. "Good God, this makes it even worse. You know what this means, old friend? First, that somebody's sitting on sacks of grain and doesn't know what he really has. But worse, I'd say we're not the only ones who've figured this out by now. They know damn well they'd not be stealing their own shipments."

"Which means we won't be the only ones trying to track down those grain sacks."

"It means more than that. It means they'll be desperate. They'll move with force, somehow, someway," Canyon said.

"What kind of real force could they have up here?" Fargo questioned.

"I don't know, but I know they're desperate for that British gold. Look at all they set up to get it through. They need it if there's going to be a secession. And they'll have a backup plan, you can be sure of it," Canyon said.

"Captain Billy expects to pick up another grain shipment in Winona, as usual," Fargo said.

"You saying we take over that shipment right there?"

"Hell, no. We'd lose the one chance to get to the rest of the grain. That shipment will be our beacon. We have to let it go through as usual. Only this time we have to be ready for the raid and follow them closely."

"By waiting on shore when they bring the sacks back."

"Probably. I haven't planned that far yet," Fargo said.

"I'm still worried about what the southern boys are going to do. Maybe they figure to do just what we're thinking about. We could be in big trouble then."

"I'm betting you're wrong about that. I'm betting they've done everything they can and they've nothing left now and they're in a damn panic. I'm going to talk to Captain Billy. The time might be at hand for you to drop your gambling-man cover. I think Billy ought to know that he's sitting on a damn keg of dynamite, that there's a hell of a lot more than stolen grain here. And we also might need his cooperation to bring this off."

"I agree, but not yet. Tell him you've some new thinking about it. Keep it at that a little while longer. We're going to get off at the next stop and do some scouting while he sails on," Canyon said.

"That'd be Moline. We ought to reach there by midday, I'd guess. Meanwhile, why don't you come visit Billy with me? I'll give you the credit for my new thinking, seeing as how I won't have any other reason to give him," Fargo said, and Canyon started to climb toward the wheelhouse with him.

They had reached the second deck when Darlene stepped from an inside corridor in Levi's and a white shirt. Her wide mouth broke into a smile, but her eyes held shrewd appraisal.

"My goodness, you two have become real pals, haven't you?" she commented.

Fargo smiled back. "He's teaching me to gamble. I'm teaching him to hunt stolen sacks of grain."

"From what I hear, neither of you is doing too well," she tossed back, and walked away, a tiny laugh trailing behind her.

"Little bitch," Fargo muttered to Canyon, and led the way to the pilot house, where Ez Crawley was there beside Captain Billy.

" 'Morning," Billy said. "You just visiting or did you find something to tell me?"

"Some of both," Fargo said. "I haven't changed my mind any about somebody stealing the grain to put you in a hole. But Canyon, here, he thinks there's maybe more to it than just that."

"Such as?" Captain Billy asked with a frown.

"Haven't a handle on it yet," Canyon answered. "It's a feeling inside me."

"The captain needs more than damn feelings," Ez Crawley cut in. "You got somethin' real, then say it, mister."

Canyon smiled as he shrugged. "I will soon as I do. Right now it's just a feeling. Sorry about that. But I trust my feelings."

"I trust hard facts," Ez growled.

"Point is, I might suddenly need your cooperation, and there won't be time for explaining. Will I have it?" Fargo said.

"What kind of cooperation?"

"Can't say now. Slowing down, making a sudden stop ashore, maybe even turning around. It could be anything. If I find those sacks, there's no saying what I might have to do to hang on to them."

"You ask and I'll go along," Billy said. "You're trying to help me. And I appreciate your help, too, O'Grady."

"Gives me something to do besides play cards," Canyon said. He included Crawley in his wave as he followed Fargo out of the pilot house and down to the deck below.

"Ez Crawley was sure interested in whether you had any hard facts," Fargo said. "He could be the southern agent on board."

"I'd be more inclined to pick Darlene," Canyon said, and Fargo frowned. "I read Crawley as loyal to Captain Billy. I think he was being protective. Besides, he's just not the type they'd pick as an agent."

"Maybe that's just why they did. Money talks. He could be their man and still be loyal to the captain."

"No, he's too much in the limelight, too easy to suspect," Canyon said. "But Darlene, she's damn sharp and she can get around more places in more ways. But we could be wrong about both of them." He shrugged and paused at the door to the corridor. "See you at the stable when we reach Moline," he said.

Fargo nodded as he hurried on to Caroline's cabin.

She looked up from a ledger book as he entered, her breasts pressed against a gray shirt and the rest of her compact figure encased in a fringed brown skirt. She rose and wrapped herself around him at once, her lips as sweetly soft as he'd remembered.

"Just came from Captain Billy. Ez was in the wheelhouse, too," he said, and told her of the conversation and of Canyon's seemingly unfocused thoughts.

"You know what he's thinking about?" she asked.

"Not rightly," he said, and swore slightly at the need to be two-faced. He trusted Caroline and wanted to confide in her. She was probably the only really open, sincere person on the boat. But he knew he'd respect Canyon's caution. The real meat of it had become his show now. "I'll be riding out from Moline with Canyon," he said. "Probably won't be back till tomorrow. I'd guess we'll meet the boat at Dubuque."

"Going to look for the sacks again?" she asked, and he nodded. "I'll go with you."

"Not this time. Stay here and put Captain Billy's mind at rest."

She gave a half-pout. "We won't reach Moline for at least another hour," she said, moved past him, and pulled the door latch shut. Her hand had begun to unbutton the gray shirt as she turned back to him, and by the time she finished, he was stripped and waiting on the bed for her. Caroline half-ran to him, fell onto his already throbbing maleness, and rolled across the small bed with him. Canyon O'Grady would have some quotation on the pursuit of pleasure at this moment, Fargo thought, but he could only think of one he had learned a long time ago: never turn down good whiskey or a warm woman, Fargo recalled as his lips found one high, round breast.

The hour passed too quickly, but it wasn't till he felt the paddle wheel slow its churning and heard the shouts of crewmen handling the mooring lines that he pulled himself from Caroline's arms. He freshened up, dressed, and paused to caress her breasts for a moment as she uttered a sigh that was a combination of pleasure and protest.

"Good luck," she called out, and sat up as he reached the door.

"We'll be needing some of that," he tossed back, and hurried from the cabin.

Canyon was waiting at the gangplank with the palomino and the Ovaro.

Fargo glimpsed Ez Crawley watch as he rode from the boat beside Canyon. "Where do we start scouting?" he asked as they trotted past the stores and sheds.

"If there was a contact made when he stopped at Keokuk, I'd say we go south," Canyon answered, turned the palomino, and set off at a canter.

Fargo rode beside him into the open country, through a low stretch of land where he saw only jackrabbits and grouse. "What are you looking for?" he asked.

"Ah, my friend, you've a way of asking difficult questions," Canyon said. "I don't know. One or more riders in a big hurry, empty wagons traveling hard, anything that catches the eye."

"I'll ride the high land to the left. You do the same on the right. That way we'll be able to cover more territory. We can stay in sight of each other. Either of us sees anything, we give a wave," Fargo suggested.

"Good enough," Canyon agreed, and sent the palomino galloping across to where a lay of high land rose, sparsely topped by mulberry trees.

Fargo turned and rode up onto the uneven ridge at his left, climbing to the top, from where he could survey the terrain below with ease. Canyon, now a small figure on the distant heights, kept pace with the Trailsman as he moved south.

As the day wore on Fargo spotted a couple in a surrey, then later, two placer miners with all their gear and two overloaded mules. Still later, he slowed to watch three men riding slowly along a road and moved on when he saw them pass a jug of whiskey among themselves. He flicked a glance across at Canyon every few minutes.

The day continued to wear on when he suddenly reined to a halt as he saw Canyon's arm wave. He put the pinto into a gallop down the slope and raced across the low land and up the other ridge. The sun had reached the distant horizon, he noted as he came up beside Canyon and immediately saw the horsemen riding below.

All were clad in work outfits, chaps, Levi's, shirts, stetsons and ten-gallon hats casually pushed back on their heads. Fargo counted some twenty-six riders. "I'd guess cowpokes on their way to a roundup," he said. "Or trailhands coming back from a drive."

"They'd pass for any of those things," Canyon said, his lips edging a slow smile. "Powerful indeed is the empire of habit, so said the old Greek philosopher Syrus."

"Habit?" Fargo echoed.

"You ever see trailhands or cowpokes ride in a column of twos?" Canyon asked, and Fargo felt a smile touch his lips.

"No, never did, now that you mention it," he said.

"Exactly. They ride in bunches, uneven clusters, or straggle out. But you know who does ride in a column of twos," Canyon said.

"A cavalry troop."

"They changed clothes but forgot to change habits," Canyon said. "Let's ride down for a closer look." He sent Cormac down the slope and Fargo came up alongside him as they crossed in front of the line of riders and came to a halt.

A young, handsome, square-jawed man at the head

of the line of riders reined up and Fargo took in the big man on a bay a few feet to one side, a wide face and brows so thick and bushy they seemed in a perpetual frown.

" 'Afternoon, gents. We've gotten ourselves turned around," Canyon said. "We're looking to get to Keokuk."

"South," the young man replied. "Ride east till you reach the river and follow it south. That's your surest way of finding it."

"Much obliged," Fargo put in, nodded pleasantly, and followed Canyon in a slow trot across the level land till they turned behind a stand of hackberry that hid them from the column of riders. They halted and peered out to watch the column move north in the fast-gathering dusk.

"They're our boys. I'll wager on it," Canyon said. "But I want to find out more. It'll be dark soon and they'll camp. Maybe we can get hold of one of them."

"Good enough. We'll just hang back and wait," Fargo said, and led the way to the top of a knoll that let them watch the column of riders wind its way north. When they were distant enough, he moved down to the flat land and followed the hoofprints still visible in the dusk.

"Damn, I still can't believe there's a disguised southern platoon up here," Fargo muttered. "Maybe they're just well-trained hired hands."

"Maybe, but I'm betting otherwise," Canyon said. "Insurance in case something went wrong with the gold shipments. It means too much not to have a backup."

"They'll be in real trouble if they're found out," Fargo said.

"They're here to do their job and then hightail it back to Missouri or wherever they're from," Canyon said. "They do it fast and right, there's no chance anybody'll find out who they are."

Fargo motioned for silence and drew to a halt. Night had descended, but he saw the darker shapes spread out on a flat circle of land. "They're bedding down. No campfires. Cold rations. We'll give them time to go into hard sleep." He dismounted and relaxed against the trunk of a small, stumpy hawthorn and let the hours go by.

The moon was nearly in the midnight sky when he rose and Canyon pushed to his feet.

"That one alone off to the left," Canyon murmured.

Fargo nodded and drew the double-edge throwing knife from the calf holster around his leg. He dropped to his belly, glanced across to see Canyon do the same, and began to inch his way along the ground. The few dozen yards seemed to stretch into a half-mile as he crept in careful silence, but the sleeping figure finally took shape in front of him. He saw a young boy's face, smooth-cheeked, looking even younger in sleep. He exchanged nods with Canyon, brought the knife up as Canyon's hand clamped down over the boy's mouth.

The sleeper's eyes snapped open, panic instant in them that turned to fear as he felt the sharp tip of the knife blade against his throat. Together, Fargo and Canyon began to pull the young boy along the ground, Canyon's one hand clamped over his mouth, the other dragging him by one arm. Fargo kept the knife blade at his throat while pulling him by the other arm. They inched their way along, keeping their hold on the boy as they dragged him ever so slowly and quietly. It seemed to take all night to go a hundred yards. They halted and Canyon pulled his hand from the boy's mouth. Fargo kept the point of the knife against his throat as the young man pushed himself to a sitting position, his eyes still round with fear.

"How old are you, boy?" Canyon asked. "Talk in whispers."

"Eighteen," the youth said.

"You want to see nineteen?" Canyon asked, and the young man nodded. "I'd like that, too, sonny. All you have to do is answer our questions." The youth nodded and Canyon smiled back. "Don't lie. My friend here can smell when a man's lying, and it makes him mad. He kills people that lie to him." The youth nodded again, threw a blinking glance at Fargo, and swallowed hard. "Now, who are you, sonny?" Canyon inquired.

"Robert Billings," the youth said.

"No, not yourself, lad. We want to know about the outfit you're riding with. Who are you?" Canyon said. "We know you're not what you make out to be."

The young man looked at the tip of the knife blade held at his throat and Fargo kept his face sullen. "First Mississippi Rifles, sir," he murmured. "Troop C."

"That'd be a cavalry outfit, right?" Canyon said, and the boy nodded. "Now, it's too early for you to be going to a Halloween party, so why are you up here all dressed like cowhands?" O'Grady asked.

"I don't know, sir. I guess because we're not supposed to be here," the youth said.

"We know that, sonny. What are you doing here?" Canyon frowned.

"I don't know. That's the truth," the youth said.

"How long have you been here?" Fargo cut in.

"We were sent up two months ago. We've been bivouacked near Oskaloosa, just waiting and waiting. I don't know for what."

"Then you got orders to move," Fargo pressed.

"Yesterday," the youth said.

"Who's your commanding officer?" Canyon asked.

"Lieutenant Williams."

"Who's the man riding along, the one with the thick, bushy eyebrows?" Fargo asked.

"His name's Fullerton. He came with the orders for us to move," the young man said.

Fargo and Canyon exchanged a quick glance and Canyon stepped back, drew the ivory-gripped Colt from its holster, and with a lightning-quick motion brought it down hard on the boy's skull.

"Sorry, lad. That's just to keep you quiet till we put some distance between us and your troop," he said as the youth fell back with a dull thud.

Fargo rose, returned the blade to the calf holster, and followed Canyon in a crouching run to where they had left the horses. "You were right all the way," he said. "A standby force, waiting in case they were needed."

"Their agent on the boat met with Fullerton and they figured out what was happening at pretty much the same time we did," Canyon said. "Fullerton put the standby force into action to try to find their gold. It's all they have left to do. We were really surprised when we figured it out. They must be spitting nails."

"You figure we'll just tag along and see if they find it?" Fargo asked, and Canyon nodded. "I'll be damned if I can see how they will. I was on the tail of it, and it disappeared into thin air on me."

"They probably won't, but I'd like to see for myself—for now, anyway," Canyon said, and led the horses under a low-branched bitternut. "Let's rest some. They'll be riding, come dawn, and we want to stay with them."

Fargo nodded, tethered the Ovaro on a loose rein, to give him room to enjoy the good crested wheatgrass that grew profusely along the way. He drew sleep to himself and didn't wake till morning touched the land. After he rose and freshened up with his canteen, he led the way upland, from where he could see the column of riders below and beyond.

The officer led his disguised cavalry troop into a dip of land, halted, and gave orders. A moment later, half the column turned west.

"He's split his men in two to cover more territory," Fargo muttered. "You take the half that went west. I'll stay with the lieutenant. I'm sure they'll be making a wide circle. We'll meet again when they do."

Canyon waved and sent the palomino after the riders heading west, and Fargo slowly followed the other half of the troopers north. He stayed in tree cover, held to high land, and hung back far enough so he could keep the column in sight. He halted as they came to a ranch, and he watched them march the family into the front yard while they thoroughly searched the main house and all the outbuildings. He followed as they moved on, and watched as they came to another ranch and did the same.

The next stop was a farmer's place with a barn full of corn, and Fargo watched them hold the farmer and three hands to one side as they searched the house and corn barn and finally moved on. They searched some dozen places they came upon as they rode northward, and he gave them credit for two things: they were firm but polite—no nonsense but no roughness. They were a well-disciplined lot, he decided.

The afternoon had begun to wane when he glimpsed the other half of the column come into sight and rejoin the lieutenant's men. It was plain they had found no gold either. They talked for a few minutes, then rode on again in a single column, the lieutenant at the head and Fullerton riding to one side.

Fargo stayed back as they rode almost out of sight; he waited and finally spied Canyon detach himself from a cluster of shagbark hickory. He spurred the Ovaro forward, let Canyon see him, and waited as the flame-headed figure rode up to him. "Zero so far, which is what I expected," Fargo said.

"Searching the houses was an off-chance they couldn't afford not to take," Canyon said. "They're on their way to something else, I'm sure. Meanwhile, they didn't want to pass up getting lucky."

"On their way to what?" Fargo questioned.

"I don't know, but they're riding north. Maybe all the way to Winona. I'd guess they'll be getting new orders there, probably at a drop somewhere," Canyon said. "We know the boat is picking up another shipment of grain sacks at Winona. Captain Billy told us that. I'm sure they expect that, too."

"You figure they plan to guard the shipment?" Fargo frowned. "How?"

"I don't know what they're planning, but I'll wager the shipment is somehow involved," Canyon answered. "Let's get on to Dubuque. I've got to get back to the boat. If I spend much more time with you, somebody's going to get suspicious. I don't want my cover blown now when we're getting close."

"Let's go. The *Shady Lady* ought to be there by now," Fargo said, and set off in a gallop, slowing only when the buildings of Dubuque rose up in front of him. Canyon beside him, the Trailsman moved through the outlying part of town to the dockside, where the *Shady Lady*'s twin smokestacks rose high above everything else. He dismounted and took Canyon's offer to stable the horses. Fargo halted at the edge of the gangplank and let his eyes sweep the boat. He saw Monica at the rail of the upper deck and watched her turn away, disapproval and anger in the gesture. Canyon's charm was in danger of being overused soon, Fargo reflected.

Caroline appeared, waved excitedly at him, and he nodded back, then brought his gaze up to the wheelhouse, where he saw Captain Billy at the side window.

His eyes moved down again and he watched passengers moving along the decks. Darlene appeared, in her white-aproned working outfit, heels clattering along the deck. His eyes went down to the main deck and scanned the crewmen coiling lines and tending to their respective chores.

Canyon returned from the stable and Fargo spoke to him as his gaze continued to sweep the boat. "I don't see Ez Crawley anywhere," he muttered.

"Maybe he's inside someplace," Canyon suggested.

"When everybody else is out getting ready to sail?" Fargo questioned, and saw Captain Billy leave the wheelhouse and come down the outside ladder.

"You find anything, Fargo?" the captain asked.

"No," Fargo said. "We sailing soon?"

"Another half-hour or so," Billy said.

"We waiting for Ez? I noticed he's not aboard," Fargo asked casually.

"No, Ez is going to meet up with us in Winona tomorrow. He has a great-aunt north of here. She had word waiting for him when we docked. Seems she has to move and needs his help. She's an old lady," Billy said.

"I didn't know Ez had a horse on board," Fargo said.

"He doesn't. He'll have to pick one up. He only left a few minutes ago," Billy said, and broke off further conversation to bark at two crewmen who were working on a torn piece of deck planking.

"I'll be back before we sail. I've a hunch I want to follow through on," Fargo muttered to Canyon, and hurried across the gangplank. He strode through the waterfront streets and halted when he saw a barbershop pole with a portly figure leaning against it in a white apron. " 'Afternoon," he called out. "You're a part of this town. You know where a man can buy a wagon around here? Or rent one?"

"Sure thing. Jim Folsom's place. Go down three streets and across two. You can't miss it," the barber said, and Fargo gave him his thanks as he hurried on. He broke into a trot, ducked out of the way of two men carrying a heavy crate, and followed the barber's directions.

The wagon outfit came into sight. Fargo saw a large, square piece of land with at least thirty wagons in it and a small corral with a half-dozen horses behind it. He slowed, and his eyes went over the wagons parked side by side. They were mostly work rigs, he noted, light farm wagons, spring wagons, open delivery wagons, and some larger seed-bed wagons and baggage rigs, but he saw a half-dozen surreys and one slightly bruised Stanhope.

Fargo started into the lot but then dropped to one knee behind one of the farm wagons as Ez Crawley came into sight from the rear of the place, a gray-haired man in overalls beside him.

"I'll have her hitched up and ready to go in five minutes," the man said as Crawley handed him a roll of bills. The man called out and a young helper appeared and the two hurried off together.

Fargo saw Ez wait with dour-faced impatience, and it was closer to ten minutes when the wagon rolled up from the back of the lot, two horses hitched to it. Fargo, peering through the spokes of the wagon wheel in front of him, took in a big Owensboro mountain wagon, the heavy-duty kind known as a California rack-bed rig with fifty-two-inch-high rear wheels. He watched Crawley climb onto the seat of the wagon, take the reins, and drive from the wagon lot.

As Crawley drove from sight with the big wagon, Fargo rose to his feet, his jaw set tight as he retraced steps to the boat. Darkness fell as he crossed the gangplank and the crewmen began to cast off mooring lines. When he reached Canyon's cabin, the boat was under way and he found the government agent putting on the ruffled shirt of his gambling-man outfit. Fargo quickly told him what he had seen, and watched the agent's lips purse in thought. "No moving an old lady aunt," Fargo said. "He wouldn't need a heavy-duty California rack bed for that."

"But six shipments of grain sacks with gold bars inside them would take a big Owensboro rig," Canyon muttered.

"You figure he's going to meet the column and turn the wagon over to them?"

"That's how I see it. Remember, they're counting

on finding those six grain shipments, and they'll need that wagon when they do."

"I wouldn't be surprised if Crawley has a lead on where the shipments might be."

Canyon shrugged. "We've nothing to do now but wait for tomorrow and Winona," he said.

"You think they'll make a move there?"

"I'd guess not. They're desperate for the gold, but they can't afford to run the risk of being caught up here. We've a brigade of federal troops just outside St. Louis, and there's Fort Atkinson not all that far away. They'll be damn careful. We watch and wait," Canyon said.

Fargo let a deep sigh escape him. "I'd say this pretty much makes Ez Crawley their agent on board," he said, and tried not to sound smug.

"It's looking that way, my friend. It most surely is," Canyon said.

Fargo smiled and accepted the concession, such as it was.

11

Dawn slid through the window of the cabin and Caroline woke, stretched, and let him enjoy the naked compact loveliness of her. He had gone to her after he'd left Canyon. She'd been full of questions and excitement, of course, and he'd told her one whole truth: that they'd found no grain sacks. The rest had been a pastiche of half-truths and evasions as she persisted in asking about why Canyon felt there was something more to the raids. He took her to bed, finally, and the questions came to an abrupt end as the body pushed aside the mind.

The night had been deliciously satisfying. Caroline's eager lovemaking reminded Fargo of a kid who'd found a wonderful new toy and couldn't put it down. But she finally slept, satiated and happy. Now she watched him from the bed as he dressed.

"You looked all day yesterday and didn't find anything. Maybe it's time to stop. Maybe it's too late," she said.

"That doesn't sound like you, honey," Fargo said.

"Well, it's not, really. It's what Captain Billy said to

me yesterday, and maybe he's right. He is very discouraged and he's still talking about giving up entirely."

"I know. He mentioned that to me. I told him to give me a little more time."

"He has, but it's just not getting anywhere."

"Maybe it is," he said, and wished he could tell her how close things really were and all that had come into the picture. "Keep the faith, baby," he said, and finished dressing.

"I'd rather keep you," she said, and sat up, the round breasts so firm they hardly swayed.

"We can work on that. I'm not going out chasing around with Canyon today. See you later," he said.

"I'll be here, finishing the books." Caroline held her arms out and he came to her, kissed her long and hard, and fought down the desire to stay.

When he hurried outside onto the deck, he saw the *Shady Lady* beginning to move into the long dock at Winona. Canyon was still sleeping. He probably had been up late playing out his role at the salon and then using more than charm to mollify Monica. Fargo strolled to the rear of the boat beside the loading gangplank, folded himself in a corner of the deck, and surveyed the broad scene in front of him.

All the passengers disembarked, he noted, and only a few new ones came aboard. Winona was plainly not a major stop for passenger traffic, but a steady parade of cargo came aboard the vessel. When three men in an unmarked wagon began to bring the sacks of grain aboard, Fargo rose and moved closer, to lean against the railing. The trio worked quickly, exchanging only a few words, but Fargo caught the heavy Canadian accents. He watched them store the grain sacks neatly in the front of the cargo area. When they finished, they paused to take a receipt from Captain Billy and quickly drove away.

Fargo sat down again, his gaze sweeping the streets that bordered the waterfront, but he saw no signs of Ez Crawley, with or without his wagon. He scanned the streets again, hoping to catch a glimpse of a column of riders. They'd be easy to spot, even if they abandoned their column formation in town.

But he saw only the usual waterfront activity and watched a river ark come in to moor, replete with a small barnyard on its stern deck.

It was midafternoon when Canyon appeared, and Fargo nodded at the instant question in his eyes. "Everything's been put aboard, all stored nice and neat in the cargo hold," he said.

"No sign of anyone else?" Canyon queried.

"No."

"Then they're waiting outside town," Canyon said, and swept the shoreline with a narrow-eyed glance.

"We just sit tight and wait to see what happens?"

"Got any better ideas?"

"Maybe we should go ashore before the boat sails and tail them again," Fargo said.

"I don't think we'll have to do that. The sacks are on board, and they know it. I don't think they'll be letting the *Shady Lady* out of their sight. Besides, I can't go ashore again tonight without getting somebody suspicious."

"You don't have to worry about that now. Their agent is ashore with his wagon," Fargo said. "Or are you telling me you're still not convinced it's Crawley?"

Canyon turned and Fargo followed his glance and saw the tall, willowy figure in the yellow dress approaching. "I'm saying my excuses are wearing thin and I'm not ready to ruin a most rewarding relationship," Canyon muttered quickly.

"Now that's something I can understand." Fargo grinned and Canyon turned to Monica as she came up to them.

"We're going ashore for what's left of the day," Canyon said. "Some shopping maybe, some looking around. A change of scenery."

"Sounds nice. Enjoy yourselves," Fargo said, and drew a warm smile from Monica. He watched Canyon cross the gangplank with her, hand in hand, and smiled to himself. Monica was the kind who would accept only so much charm. He sat back, watched Canyon and Monica disappear in the shore crowds, and relaxed in the last of the sun.

Dusk had started to drift across the river when Captain Billy came by to lean on the rail beside him. "The grain's aboard, another shipment. You think they'll raid it again?" the captain asked.

Fargo turned the question in his mind. With all that he'd discovered, he hadn't considered the question. Whoever hired the Fox to raid the shipments wouldn't know that all hell had broken loose behind the scenes. There'd be no reason for him not to raid this shipment as he had all the others. "It's likely," he said slowly, and Captain Billy uttered a bitter sound.

"Maybe this time we can stop them. I could arm some of the crew and you could get O'Grady to stand watch with you," the captain said. "It's worth a try."

"I'll talk to Canyon about it," Fargo said. "Caroline tells me you're still thinking of quitting. Give me a little more time."

Captain Billy shrugged. "Time's about the only thing I've left to give," he said, and Fargo saw the deep lines on his round face. He watched the man trudge off and disappear behind the boiler-room passage.

Darkness came and Fargo saw Canyon and Monica return, arm in arm, Monica's low, throaty laugh carrying across the deck. He waited a proper amount of time before climbing to Canyon's cabin, where he was greeted with an almost sheepish shrug.

"The things we do to keep a woman happy," Canyon said.

"And ourselves satisfied," Fargo said.

"I stand corrected." The agent laughed. He listened carefully as Fargo told him of Captain Billy's questions. "You're right," Canyon said when he finished. "There's no reason why there shouldn't be another raid on the shipment. But I'm wondering what our southern friends will be doing if there is."

"It promises to be an interesting evening," Fargo said. "I'll meet you in an hour. We'll just settle down to wait. We ought to be sailing in a few minutes," he said, and hurried down the vessel to Caroline's cabin, where she greeted him with a hug and a tired smile.

"I finished work and I'm exhausted," she said. "Expenses, bills, invoices, receipts, cash profits, I don't want to look at a ledger for another week." She stretched out on the bed, fully clothed, and he sank down beside her.

"Why aren't we sailing?" he asked aloud, and she gave a small shrug. "I'll be right back," he said, and hurried outside.

Deep darkness had closed in over everything, the daytime shorefront activities ended, and there was only the silence and the deep night. He spied Captain Billy's square figure in the wheelhouse and climbed up two steps at a time. "Problems?" he asked as he entered. "Aren't we supposed to be sailing by now?"

"Ez hasn't come back yet," Captain Billy said. "I'll give him a few more hours."

"Won't that wreck your schedule?" Fargo frowned.

"We'll be running downriver with the current. I'll be able to make it up easily."

Fargo grimaced inwardly. He wanted to tell Billy it was damned unlikely that Ez Crawley would be returning—not tonight, anyway. But he kept the words inside himself. "You know what you're doing," he said cheerfully, and hurried down to Canyon's cabin, where the agent greeted him with surprise. "No need to hurry to take up watch," he said, and told him of the exchange with Billy. "We'll be here another two hours before we even sail. I'll be with Caroline. Might as well make the most of it. I likely won't have time later."

"Maybe I can talk Monica into being late for the faro table. Meet you on deck after we've been sailing for half an hour."

Fargo nodded and returned to Caroline, who had suddenly had a return of energy. "Two hours?" she echoed with a sly smile even as she began unbuttoning her blouse. "Yes, why not make the most of it?" She whipped off clothes and came into his arms with that wonderful passionate, eager energy he had come to enjoy for itself, her firm body exploding in delight at his every touch. She turned the lamp low and let the cabin become a place of soft yellow glow and soft murmured groans until finally she lay half over him, her smooth skin a tingling blanket.

He drew his breath in and let the embers of passion cool down as her hands played tiny games of exploration across his muscled body. A soft, rocking motion drifted through his half-awake consciousness, and he suddenly sat up, Caroline sliding to the bed.

"We're sailing," he breathed.

"Some while now," she murmured. "I thought you felt it."

"I was too busy feeling other things," he said, and swung long legs over the bed and reached for clothes.

"When you sail as long as I have, you're quick to feel every little change on the boat," she said. He grunted, angry at himself, as he strapped on his gun belt. "Where will you be?" she asked.

"On deck."

"I'll come visit," Caroline said.

"No, no distractions," Fargo said brusquely. "I'll see you later. Maybe . . ." He hurried outside and found Canyon sitting against the outside cabin walls, the *Shady Lady* moving downriver in midstream.

"I was about to come rescue you," Canyon slid at him.

"You're a good man," Fargo muttered as he sank on one knee on the deck. "You might just have the right word there."

"Keep your eyes on the trees along the shore," O'Grady said.

Fargo peered through the blackness at the darker shadows of the sandbar willows that bordered the shoreline. It took him a moment to adjust his eyes to the dark, but he suddenly smiled as he found the slow-moving horsemen passing along the trees. They stayed just at the edge of the foliage, he saw.

"I checked the other side. Half of them are riding the opposite shore," Canyon said. "They're keeping up with us. They're going to make sure this shipment goes through."

"Orders Ez Crawley probably brought them," Fargo said, peering hard at the shoreline. "Take another look," he muttered, and saw Canyon lean forward to strain his eyes through the darkness.

"They're not paralleling us anymore," he said.

"They've fallen back a dozen yards. They're keeping pace but hanging back. Smart," Fargo muttered. He settled back beside Canyon and relaxed, listening to the insect sounds of the warm night.

Time moved slowly and the riverboat slowed as it rounded a curving section of the Mississippi and then sailed down a straight but narrow section. Fargo fought away the sleep-inducing motion of the boat and saw Canyon, his head back, watch the shoreline through slitted eyes.

The boat had sailed for perhaps another hour when Fargo felt it suddenly slow, the paddle wheels churning to a halt. He rose and peered forward beyond the bow. The wavy tangle of skeletonlike arms rose from the river and seemed to reach out for the prow of the boat. "A sawyer," he said to Canyon, who now stood beside him. "Captain Billy will stay till it sinks again."

"That's not all that's out there," Canyon said, and nodded toward the shoreline.

Fargo saw the dark shapes moving from the shore into the river, the canoes and rafts immediately heading for the *Shady Lady*. Each canoe held at least four silent figures.

Canyon darted to the other side of the vessel through the passageway beside the paddle-wheel housing. He returned in a moment to drop to one knee, the ivory-gripped Colt in his hand. "They're coming from the other side, too, as they did last time."

Fargo heard the clatter of footsteps and glimpsed three crewmen carrying rifles hurry across the deck. "Billy said he was going to put up a real fight this time," Fargo said.

Canyon's reply was drowned out by an explosion of gunfire from the shore and Fargo saw the riders move out of the trees. Firing carbines, they laid down a withering fusillade of shots and the figures in the barges began to topple into the river.

"What'd you say?" Fargo asked Canyon.

"Billy's not going to need to put up a fight," Canyon answered, and Fargo heard the heavy volley of gunfire from the other side of the boat. The Saux Fox in the canoes tried to fire back with arrows and guns, but they were cut down before they could take aim. Two canoes tried to flee, their occupants paddling furiously, but all were blown into the water by a volley of shots that also riddled and sank the canoe while they were still in it. The horsemen on shore continued to pour volley after volley with military precision, and in minutes the river was awash with corpses and half-sunken canoes. There was no need to go to the other side of the boat, he knew. The thunder of rifle fire had painted the same scene. The gunfire halted with abruptness and Fargo saw the riders race back into the trees. He turned to meet Canyon's eyes.

"Hard. Efficient. Complete," Canyon muttered.

Fargo turned as he heard the shouts and footsteps hurrying down from the upper decks. Captain Billy appeared first, and two of his crewmen halted behind him.

Fargo saw Caroline rush toward him and halt, shock

flooding her face as she stared at the river. "Oh, my God," she breathed, and a few passengers looked down from the upper deck.

Monica hurried down to join the others and he saw her eyes find Canyon with relief. She turned to stare at the reddened waters of the Mississippi. "Who did this? Certainly not you two," she said.

"Riders on shore," Captain Billy answered. "Two sets of them, one on each bank."

"Who were they? Where did they come from?" Caroline asked, her round face still wreathed in shock.

"They've been riding along with us," Fargo said.

"Why? Who the hell were they?" Captain Billy snapped.

Fargo met Canyon's glance and read the message in his eyes. Tell them everything but not about me, it said, and Fargo blinked understanding.

"They were the First Mississippi Rifles, Troop C," Fargo said, and saw Darlene arrive to gather around with the others.

"The what?" Captain Billy frowned.

"A troop of southern cavalry up here disguised as cowhands," Fargo said.

"How do you know that?" Monica asked.

Fargo held back his answer for a moment as he chose words. "Came onto one of them when I was scouting. I got him to talk," he said, and saw Monica accept the answer.

"Why?" Caroline put in. "Why are they up here and riding along with us?"

"Because those shipments are a lot more than what they seem to be," Fargo said. "There are gold bars inside them. They've all had gold bars in them."

Captain Billy stared at him. "What kind of damn-fool talk is this, Fargo?"

"No damn-fool talk, Billy. I didn't know about it either, at first," Fargo said.

"You figured somebody was having the shipments stolen to get to me, staging it to make it look like they were just Indian raids." The captain frowned. "You change your mind about that?"

"No, I'm still right about that. I just didn't know the whole of it then," Fargo said. "The South has been smuggling British gold in on the *Shady Lady*, and the gold has been hidden in the grain sacks."

"All having nothing to do with the raids on the grain shipments," Captain Billy said.

"That's right. Whoever has the grain sacks doesn't know what he really has. He thinks he's got grain shipments."

"Good God," Billy breathed, his eyes staring.

"How'd you come to know all this?" Monica asked.

"My own sources," Fargo said, and hoped the answer would be enough for her. He turned to Billy again. "There's more, I'm afraid. The South has had an agent aboard your boat for the last few months. They also set up a fake haulage-and-warehouse operation to receive the shipments in St. Louis, everything to ensure getting the shipments through."

"Then somebody started raiding and stealing the grain," the captain followed.

"That's right." Fargo nodded. "As I piece it together, their agent on board thought their own people were pulling off the raids for some reason or other. I figure they didn't realize what was happening till just about the same time I did. When they figured out the truth of it, they had to move quick to try to do something about the stolen grain shipments."

"And protect the one being shipped now," Caroline put in, and Fargo nodded.

"Their agent on board, you know who it is, Fargo?" Captain Billy asked.

"Ez Crawley," Fargo said, and watched the captain's jaw drop open.

"No, no, you've got to be wrong there. I can't believe that," the captain protested.

"Believe it. I've been watching him, tailing him. That's the reason for all the times he's gone ashore on one excuse or another," Fargo said.

"He has made an unusual amount of shore trips lately," Billy admitted. "But I still can't believe it. Ez has been with me a mighty long time."

"They offered him a chance to make some real money—an extra job, you might say," Fargo answered.

"All those stolen grain sacks with gold bars inside them, held by somebody who doesn't know it. Ez Crawley a southern agent. I'm having trouble believing any of it, Fargo," the captain said.

"I can fix that quickly enough," Fargo said as he spun and strode to the cargo area, the others following on his heels. He took a caulking hook with its sharp, curved end from a wall peg and sliced the first sack open. The grain spilled onto the floor to make a small mound. He reached into the more or less empty sack, probed with his hand, and found only more grain. He slashed the second sack open and again the grains of wheat spilled out, but only wheat. He frowned as he ripped a third sack open, then another and still another. None held anything but the wheat that spilled from them. His glance at Canyon was too quick for any of the others to notice. Canyon's eyes returned only helpless consternation.

"There's no gold in these sacks, Fargo. What are you trying to pull off here?" the captain barked.

Fargo's lips were a thin line as thoughts raced through his head. Finally he let out a shout of triumph. "There was gold in them, dammit," he said. "During those extra two hours you waited at Winona, Ez Crawley stole aboard, took the gold bars out of the sacks, and retied each one. He probably had to make two or three trips, but nobody was on watch then, you know that," he said to the captain.

"That's true enough," Billy murmured.

"He could carry off the gold bars without trouble, and he had a heavy Owensboro wagon waiting. I saw him buy it," Fargo said.

"Why? Why not just let the shipment go through?" Billy questioned.

"They'd had six shipments raided, and now they know it was somebody else doing it, they wanted to be sure to protect this one. So Ez took the gold bars out of the sacks," Fargo explained.

"Something doesn't make sense, Fargo," Caroline interrupted. "If they knew the gold wasn't in the sacks, why did they butcher the Indians? Why did they ride along and wait for the raid?"

"They expect to bring more shipments through. They did two things at once: removed the gold and sent a message. I expect it'll be damn hard for anyone to hire the Fox to make any more raids after this," Fargo said.

"So they'll be able to go on smuggling gold in the grain sacks without more raids," Caroline said.

"I believe Fargo's just about got it all straight," Canyon said, and Fargo tried not to look grateful.

Captain Billy slouched against the rail beside Caroline, his round face drained. "Gold inside grain shipments, Ez Crawley a southern agent, all this going on under my nose and I never knew it. I must be real dumb."

"Don't blame yourself. I went back and forth on it a few times before I could put it together," Fargo said.

"Not all the pieces," Caroline cut in. "Somebody staged the raids and stole the shipments to get at Captain Billy. We still don't know who that is."

"I'm betting we'll find that answer when we find the grain sacks that are missing," Fargo said.

"Those southern troopers could find them first," Monica said. "Or what if neither of you find them? What if whoever took them just threw them away someplace, not knowing what was in them?"

Fargo's lips drew back in distaste. "I don't want to think about any of those things yet."

Fargo saw Captain Billy straighten up, a tired, drained figure.

"I heard everything you said. I saw those riders massacre the Fox. I guess it all fits. I just can't bring myself to believe it, especially about Ez," Billy said, his voice weary. "I've got to get back to the wheel. That's sawyer's dropped down. We can go on now." He turned and climbed the steps to the pilot house and Fargo watched the others begin to drift away. Monica left with Canyon and Darlene was the last to turn and go inside the boat.

He felt Caroline's hand steal into his. "Come back to the cabin with me. I'm still in a daze over this," she said.

"I'll meet you there in a few minutes," he told her, and she walked away slowly. When she was gone, he hurried up to Canyon's cabin. In the hallway, he ducked back into an open cabin doorway as he saw Monica leaving the agent's cabin. She passed him, heels clicking along the wood floor, and he let her fade from earshot before he stepped into the hallway again.

Canyon opened at his knock and Fargo slipped into the cabin. "Figured you'd be stopping by. I sent Monica on to the faro table, not that she felt much like it. She'll deal a few games and then close up shop and come back here," Canyon said. "You did real well down there. Not finding the damn gold really threw you, I'm sure. It did me."

"It had to be Crawley sneaking back while we were at Winona," Fargo said.

"I agree." Canyon nodded. "Where do we go from here?"

"I'm going ashore, come morning, and try to find him before he meets up with the others. He can't make too much time in that heavy Owensboro. He might even stop to sleep some. Right now Troop C is still riding along with the boat. If they stop and turn inland, you go ashore and tail them. They might have a meeting place with Crawley set up. If so, we'll be there, too."

"All right. There's a good chance they may both be headed for St. Louis," Canyon said.

"We'll see," Fargo said, and hurried away down the corridors to Caroline's cabin.

She hugged him to her and sat down on the edge of the bed with him, shock still clinging to her pug-nosed face. "It's all too much, too sudden. I haven't really taken it all in yet," she said. "But I've been thinking

206

one thing: maybe Monica is right, maybe nobody will ever find those six stolen shipments."

Fargo grunted at what he was beginning to realize was a distinct possibility, and he thought of how Canyon would see it. "In a way, the end result will be the same. The South will be the big losers, all that gold gone and their St. Louis setup exposed."

Caroline frowned into space. "I suppose so. But if we found it, would it belong to us?"

"Not much chance of that, honey." Fargo laughed. "The government will claim it as contraband. And be damned happy to get it, of course."

Caroline lay back across the bed and pulled him down beside her as she stared up at the cabin ceiling. "I still can't understand how those sacks of grain just disappeared that night we followed the Saux Fox," she said. "They weren't just whisked into thin air or swallowed up by the river."

"You're right," he agreed, echoing the frustration in her voice. The sacks hadn't been whisked into thin air or swallowed up by the river: the words continued to dance a mocking rigadoon in his head. Then suddenly, like an imperious dance master, he brought the dance to an abrupt halt and a frown slid across his brow. He sat up, and suddenly the words were dancing through his head again, an excited polka this time. "That's it," he shouted at Caroline as she sat up with him.

"What's it?"

"They weren't whisked into thin air or swallowed up by the river. But how about a lake? They had the sacks in the wagon waiting by the river. We were right about that. And we found where they met the other wagon."

"We thought they'd transferred the sacks to it, but they hadn't." Caroline nodded.

"That's right. But where did they meet?" Fargo pressed.

"Beside that lake," Caroline said, her eyes widening.

"That's why there was no transfer. They put the sacks in the lake," Fargo said, and felt the excitement swirling inside him. "It's the perfect hiding place, but it never came to me till just now. You triggered it."

"It never occurred to me either," Caroline said.

"We were too caught up wondering where they'd transferred the sacks," Fargo said. "But I'm going back there and see if I'm right."

"We're going back," Caroline corrected firmly.

"I'd best do this one alone."

"Why? There's less danger now than when I followed the Fox with you. We didn't know what we'd run into then," she said with a kind of logic he couldn't refute.

"True enough," he said, his own thoughts coming together. "And if I'm right you can hightail it back and get Canyon."

"All right," she agreed.

"I've got to get Captain Billy to do what I want. He'll have a cat fit if you go," Fargo said.

"I'll worry about that," Caroline said.

He was at the door in one long stride. "Stay here. I'll be back for you," he said, and ran to Canyon's cabin. He breathed a sigh of relief to see that Canyon was still alone. "I think I know where the missing shipments may be," he blurted out, and quickly repeated his thoughts. "If I'm wrong, we've lost nothing but some extra riding," he finished.

"It's sure worth a try," Canyon agreed. "I wanted

to stay aboard and see where the Mississippi boys went, but I'll go with you."

"No need. I'm taking Caroline. I expect we'll reach the lake by dawn. If she's not back in two hours or so after daybreak, something's wrong. You can come after us then," Fargo said. "That raid was made north of Muscatine. The lake is farther north, some ten miles inland near Minnesota Territory. It's the biggest one in the area, oblong, with irregular shorelines on both sides. You can't miss it from high ground."

"I'll find it," Canyon said.

Fargo hurried from the cabin and went to the wheelhouse, where a young crewman stood beside Captain Billy at the wheel. Both men turned to look at him as he entered. "Time for your help, Billy," the Trailsman said. "I'm going ashore."

"What for?" The captain frowned.

"I think I might know where the missing grain shipments are hidden," Fargo said. "That lake near Minnesota Territory."

Captain Billy stared back at him. "You keep coming up with one surprise notion after another. Now, where'd you get that one?"

"I should've put it together long ago, but I didn't. But I think I'm right and I aim to find out," Fargo said. "I want you to stay in midriver but slow the boat almost to a standstill and lower the gangplank into the water."

"You're going to walk your horse into the river," Billy said.

"You've got it. The Mississippi boys are still riding along the shore. I don't want any splashing sounds reaching them. Once I'm in the water, I'll swim upriver with the Ovaro," Fargo said.

"Whatever you say, Fargo, but it sounds to me like you're chasing rainbows."

"Maybe, but I'm going to chase them. I'll get saddled up."

"Go down and get the gangplank ready for lowering," Billy said to the crewman.

Fargo hurried to the stable to find Caroline there with both horses saddled and ready.

"You tell him I was going?" she asked.

"No," he said as he felt the boat slow almost to a halt and saw the crewmen extend the gangplank into the water. "Let's go." He led the Ovaro forward.

Captain Billy's short, square figure waited beside the gangplank and Fargo watched the man's face explode as he saw Caroline. "What are you doing here?" the captain barked.

"Going with Fargo," she said.

"No, you're not," he bellowed. "You looking to get yourself killed?"

"I'm looking to help you, Billy. I can help find those grain sacks," Caroline said.

"You've done enough. This has turned into something really big. There's too much involved now, according to Fargo. It's too dangerous, the stakes too high. I don't want you in it," Billy said.

"I brought Fargo in. I want to see it through with him," Caroline said, her feisty stubbornness rising.

"No, forget about it. I'm just a small part of it now. What happens to me is unimportant," Billy threw back. "I don't even really care anymore. I just want you safe."

"You're tired and discouraged. You've been under a lot of strain. You're not thinking clearly, about me or yourself. I'll be safe with Fargo," Caroline said, and led her horse across the gangplank.

"Damn your stubborn hide, Caroline Hopkins," Billy called after her as she hurried forward.

Fargo grasped hold of her mount's cheek strap. "Slow down nice and slow. Ease your horse into the water. Watch me." He sent the Ovaro down the gangplank, walked beside the horse into the river until he felt the gangplank no longer under his feet. He began to swim and felt the Ovaro begin to paddle a few moments later. Keeping a grip on the horse's cheek strap, he guided the Ovaro into midriver.

Caroline followed him into the water with the same careful slowness he had used. He waited till he saw the horse swimming beside her and turned to make his way soundlessly through the dark water. He could hear the riders on shore. They had slowed, but they were still moving on. He heard the paddle wheel slowly start to turn.

Caroline swam a few yards behind him beside her horse as he stayed in midriver and felt the current pull at him. He went on for perhaps another quarter-mile before he turned and swam to the west bank and climbed out of the river. He was in the saddle when Caroline emerged and he reached down and helped her climb onto her mount.

"Let's go. It'll be morning damn soon," Fargo said, and put the pinto into a fast trot through the night, Caroline riding beside him. He turned to high land as morning neared, and when the first gray light broke, he could see the terrain below and ahead. He spotted the large, oblong lake with the irregular shoreline in the distance and hurried the pinto downward. He and

Caroline reached the lake just as the sun broke over the water.

He edged the bank until he reined to a halt. "This is the spot." He pointed to the ground. "The wagon tracks are still there."

He leapt to the ground, unstrapped his gun belt, and let it drop. He stripped off clothes and moved into the lake. Caroline watched from the shore as he reached deeper water and turned to toss a wave at her.

The new sun began to penetrate the surface of the lake. The Trailsman rose in the water and plunged beneath the surface of the cool lake water. He plunged downward and struck out more deeply and still more deeply. The water grew clouded as he continued to plunge downward. He felt his chest tighten as breath began to fade away. He was about to turn and head for the surface when he suddenly saw the dark, unformed mass directly below him.

He felt his chest beginning to hurt as his breath supply drew to an end, but he pushed himself another few feet downward, unsure whether the shape below him was a rock or some underwater formation at the bottom. He reached out with both hands and his fingers touched the shape, moved along the unmistakable texture of burlap. He managed to grin with his mouth closed and struck upward for the surface, his chest burning as if it were being constricted. He shot out of the water just as it seemed his lungs were about to burst; he gasped in a deep breath and shook the lake from his face.

Caroline was at the water's edge, concern on her round-cheeked face.

"I found them," he shouted as he let himself tread water. "They're there on the bottom, all of them."

"My God," Caroline breathed.

"Things seem lighter in water. I'll try to bring one up," Fargo said, and disappeared under the lake surface. With no need to explore, his descent was faster, and the sacks of grain took shape again as he reached the bottom. He took hold of a sack at the end of the small mountain of burlap, pulled, and it came loose. He gathered it into his arms and used his powerful leg muscles to propel himself up until he burst to the surface holding the sack to his chest.

"Over here. Bring it over here," a voice called out, but it was not Caroline's voice.

Fargo blinked water from his eyes, brought his gaze to the shore, and saw the dour face of Ez Crawley, a big Remington carbine in his hands.

12

Fargo's eyes snapped from Ez Crawley to find Caroline. He saw her sitting on her hands a few feet away.

"Over here with that," Crawley called out again, and Fargo waded through the shallow water and dropped the sack onto the sandy bank.

"Ez Crawley, what's got into you?" Caroline asked.

"Shut up, Miss Caroline," the man barked as he kept the big Remington trained on Fargo. "Get over there by her," he ordered.

"Mind if I put my pants on?" Fargo said, and started to reach down for his things.

The rifle barked and sent a spray of sand into the air an inch from his hand.

"Get away from there," Crawley snapped, and Fargo pulled back. Ez stepped forward, picked up the Trailsman's gun belt and holster, and flung both into the edge of the line of willows just back from the water. He followed with the throwing knife in its calf holster, kicked through Fargo's clothes, and stepped back. He motioned with his head and Fargo came forward again, scooped up the Levi's and pulled them on. He glimpsed the big Owensboro partly obscured by the tree leaves as he lowered himself to the ground near Caroline.

"We know all about it now, Ez," Caroline said. "It's not too late to stop. I know Captain Billy would forgive you."

Crawley's dark and dour face frowned at her. "You know what you're talking about, girl?" he asked.

"About their hiring you as an agent for them. We know all about it," Caroline said. "Fargo put it together.

Ez Crawley turned a grimace of a smile at Fargo. "Isn't he the smart one," the man growled.

Fargo felt the furrow slide across his forehead as he peered at Crawley. "Something's wrong here," he murmured aloud to Caroline. "He's pulling something."

"Go ahead, let's hear all of it, smart-ass," Crawley growled.

"You knew the sacks had been dumped here. You must have followed the Fox after one of the first raids and saw them dump them. But you didn't tell your southern friends, did you?" Fargo said, and a harsh smile slid across his face as he spoke to Caroline with his eyes on Crawley. "He's going to double-cross the southern boys. He's going to let them finish their searching and go back empty-handed and take the gold for himself," Fargo finished.

"Wrong again," a voice cut in, and Fargo half-spun to see a short figure emerge from the trees leading a horse behind him. He heard Caroline's gasp of surprise and excitement.

"Billy," she cried out.

Fargo started to get to his feet when he saw Captain Billy point a Savage and North navy revolver at him, his finger on the ring trigger that cocked the gun and rotated the cylinder.

"Don't move, Fargo," Billy said, his round face surprisingly hard.

"What the hell is this?" Fargo frowned and felt the confusion sweep through him.

"It's final reckoning time for you, Fargo," Captain Billy said. "You know, as I listened to you explain everything after the raid, I said to myself, Now there's a man with a way of figuring the right things out wrong and the wrong things out right."

Fargo stared at Billy and the confusion inside him changed to incredulousness and then to bitter realization. "You," he said. "You all the way, behind the raids, planning everything. You and Crawley working together, hiring the Saux Fox and paying them with the whiskey after they dumped the sacks here."

"You see, you can get things right if you try," Captain Billy sneered.

"Billy, what's he saying? He's not right, is he?" Caroline broke in, and started to push to her feet.

"Stay there, dammit," Captain Billy barked at her, and she fell back onto the sand. "You've been a damn problem all along, Caroline," he accused. "I'll talk to you more later."

"It's true," Caroline breathed, plainly unable to fully accept what she realized. "It was you, Billy. It was you."

"Yes, dammit," the captain snapped angrily. "Truth is, it all started by accident. One of the sacks in the first shipment came open and Ez and I found the gold bars inside it. We knew what the shipments were right then and there. Of course, we didn't know who was shipping them or why."

"You found that out last night when I told you after the raid," Fargo said.

"That's true. You had that part right, I realized," Captain Billy said.

"You old bastard. You were so shocked about your good friend Ez being a southern agent," Fargo bit out.

"Wasn't I, though? I had trouble not laughing at that," the man said. "Of course, I never knew they had an agent on board. Wonder who it is, not that it matters any, now."

Canyon had been right about Ez Crawley all along, Fargo thought and cast a glance at Caroline. She stared at Captain Billy, her eyes still wide with something between shock and sadness. "Where's the boat now?" Fargo asked.

"I pulled into shore soon after you and Caroline left. I knew I couldn't let you find the sacks and ruin everything, and I wasn't sure if Ez would get here in time," the captain said. "You see, Ez and I decided this would be the last shipment. You kept talking about something bigger than someone out to ruin me, and I decided you had gotten hold of something. I figured we wouldn't risk waiting any longer to make our move."

"But you'd already hired the Fox to make the usual raid. You let that go through, but you had Ez sneak back on board and remove the gold from the shipment. That way, everything would seem as usual. And if I went off chasing them again and caught them, I'd find nothing but the grain. My little theory would stay in place."

"Bull's-eye," Captain Billy said. "Of course, I didn't know those southern boys were all set to interfere."

"There never was anyone stealing the shipments to

get at you," Caroline interjected, bitter realization in her voice now.

"No," Fargo answered with his own bitterness. "That was another place I went wrong. I thought the men who tried to kill me did so to stop me from helping Captain Billy. But they were Fullerton's boys, who didn't want anyone nosing around on board."

"Why did you let me bring Fargo in to help?" Caroline asked Billy.

"I tried to talk you out of it," the captain said.

"Yes, you did."

"You kept insisting. I figured it might look suspicious to somebody if I kept refusing help, so I went along with you. I didn't figure he'd come onto much."

"Only I did, but with a lot of the pieces in the wrong place," Fargo grunted.

"Tie his hands," Billy ordered Ez. He kept the pistol trained on Fargo as Crawley took a length of rope from the wagon and bound his wrists together. "Caroline, too," Billy said, and drew a gasp of protest from her. "For your own damn good, so you don't do anything foolish," the captain snapped.

"Thank you," Caroline said icily.

"Dammit, girl, I was going to tell you in time. You'll be a rich young lady now. There's enough for the three of us for ten lifetimes," Captain Billy said to her.

"Men have been killed because of this, Billy—men you hired, Indians you hired. Fargo was almost killed tracking the grain. Death, lies, deceit. I don't want to be rich on those terms," Caroline said.

"It's easy to have ideals when you're young," the captain grunted.

"What happens to Fargo now?" Caroline asked.

"I'm afraid I can't have anybody running around who knows about this," Billy said. "I sweated out a lifetime of work on that dammed river. I'm not doing any more of it. I'm not giving up this chance."

"I can't believe what I'm hearing," Caroline said. "This isn't you, Billy. It isn't."

"Shut up, girl. You won't have to see anything when the time comes," Billy said, turned from her, and walked to the gray horse.

Fargo watched him take a grappling hook with a long line attached from the rear of the saddle. He handed the hook to Crawley as he took the Remington from his hands. "I'll watch them. You start getting the sacks up," Billy said, and Fargo watched the dour-faced man stride into the lake, keep moving until he was in water almost up to his shoulders. He raised the big grappling hook and tossed it out farther into the water. It sank beneath the surface and Fargo saw the rope spin out and grow slack in the water as Crawley let the hook sink. He pulled on it and the rope grew taut.

"Got one," Crawley called out, and slowly pulled the rope through the water. He worked very carefully, eased the rope upward at an angle, and pulled with extreme caution. Over five minutes had passed before the sack came to the surface, the grappling hook embedded in one corner. Ez sloshed his way to the sack, removed the hook, and hoisted the grain onto his shoulder to return to the shore. He set the sack upright on the ground beside the one Fargo had brought up.

"We'll open them later. Get the rest up now," Captain Billy said, and Crawley waded back into the lake with the hook.

Fargo felt Caroline's eyes on him and turned to her.

"I'm so sorry, Fargo," Caroline murmured. "God, I'm sorry."

"Nothing's your fault," he told her.

"I brought you into this."

"For good reasons."

"You're still here, tied up and facing God knows what," she said. "I'll talk to Billy some more."

"You'll only waste your breath," Fargo said. "He's another man now—one you've never known."

"I've got to try," she said despairingly.

Fargo cast an eye at the sun. "Don't be giving up yet, honey," he murmured, and Caroline frowned back. He only smiled at her. Ez Crawley would be another hour at least getting the bags up and opened. A lot could happen in an hour.

Canyon returned to his cabin, the restless nagging premonition of trouble still inside him.

Monica leaned on one elbow across the bed, still in her long black faro dealer's gown. "You find out why we've pulled to shore?" she asked.

"A crewman told me Captain Billy decided to wait here for Fargo and Caroline to come back," Canyon answered.

"You see Billy?"

"No," he said, and sat down on the edge of the bed.

"How about the Mississippi Rifles?" Monica asked.

"They've settled down a hundred yards or so south," Canyon told her.

"You know, I still can't understand how Fargo knew about the gold shipments," Monica said. "He was chasing Indians with sacks of stolen grain. How did he find out about smuggled gold and southern agents on board?"

Canyon's lips pursed as thoughts turned in his head. There was no need for holding back any longer. If Fargo found the sacks, it would be all over. They had only to sit tight until they reached Fort Madison, where help was available. "I mean, it just doesn't add up that he'd suddenly know so much," Monica said. "Unless he's more than he says he is."

"I told him about the gold and the southern agent aboard," Canyon said, and watched Monica turn to him, a frown slowly sliding across her smooth forehead.

"You told him?" she echoed slowly.

He offered a smile that edged sheepishness. "It's not Canyon O'Grady, gambling man, lass. It's Canyon O'Grady, U.S. government agent," he said.

Monica's long stare stayed and her blue eyes seemed to peer through him. "You, a government agent?" she said finally, and Canyon nodded. "That's why you've been so busy helping Fargo," Monica said.

"Not altogether. We're old friends. Things just happened to come together," he said. "I couldn't tell you before this. There was too much still hanging fire." Monica continued to stare at him and the furrow stayed on her brow, but he saw something come into her eyes. "You look more sad than surprised," he remarked.

"I guess that's so," Monica half-shrugged. "Now I understand some of the things you tried to tell me about not making plans for us. I thought you were just being footloose and fancy-free."

"I'm sorry, Monica. You're special. But it doesn't have to end right here and now for us," Canyon said.

Her eyes studied him as though she were seeing him for the very first time. "You'll always be a gambling man to me, Canyon O'Grady," she said. "And you've certainly been very special to me. Maybe you're right. It doesn't have to end right here and now for us." Her hand came up, undid the few snaps that held the black gown in place, and in seconds she came to him in all her willowy, naked loveliness, jet-black hair falling against her pale-white skin, the full-cupped breasts touching his chest. He pulled off clothes, pushed aside the restless, silent voices inside him, and fell back on the bed with her.

Monica sighed, purred, made love slowly, her hands caressing, prolonging every moment, drawing ecstasy to its fullest. When he slid inside her warmth, her willowy body rose, twisted, thrust with him. Her cries filled the cabin until, with a final scream of utter joy, the night exploded and the entire world was contained within the four walls of the tiny cabin.

Monica lay exhausted beside Canyon. She dozed, one arm across his chest, stirred, hugged him to her, and dozed again.

O'Grady tried to sleep, but the gnawing inside him persisted, and when he suddenly saw the first gray light of dawn against the cabin window, he slid from the bed, washed, and began to dress. He was half-finished when Monica woke and sat up.

"What are you doing?" She frowned.

"Going after Fargo," Canyon said.

"Why?"

"He told me that if Caroline wasn't back in two hours after dawn to come after him," Canyon said. "But I'm not waiting. Something's wrong. I feel it in my bones."

"How do you know you'll find him?" Monica asked as she swung from the bed.

"He thinks the missing sacks are in a lake ten miles north of Muscatine and a few miles west. It's the biggest in the area. I'll find it," Canyon said. Monica went to the big basin of water, freshened up, and began to dress. "Give me a minute to change at my cabin and I'll go with you," she said. "I want to help."

"No. I've no idea what I'll be running into," Canyon said. "You be here waiting for me."

Monica returned a cool glance. "I'm sure the First Mississippi Rifles are still waiting out there," she said, and Canyon frowned back.

"Yes, you're right. All right, you can help. I don't want them to see me leave. You can create a diversion," Canyon said.

"How?"

"Take a horse from the stable and ride out past them. They'll stop you. While their attention's on you, I'll sneak ashore."

"Give me a minute to change into riding clothes," Monica said, and hurried down the corridor to her cabin.

He waited for her outside and climbed down to the stable with her as she reappeared in jeans and a tan shirt. He saddled the palomino as Monica waited, and paused beside her when he finished.

"Now, I don't want you getting yourself into trouble," he said. "Don't be smart-ass with them. Just keep their attention. Answer their questions. Tell them you decided to take a ride. And don't try to run."

Monica reached up, kissed him gently, and again he saw the sadness in her eyes. She managed a small smile as he patted her on the rear and helped her onto the horse. He waited while she rode down the gangplank and moved to where the Mississippi boys had settled down. He watched her pass their small encampment.

They came out to halt her. Four figures detached themselves from the others and hurried to where Monica sat the horse. The others were looking on, Canyon saw, and he moved down the gangplank leading the palomino by the reins. He glimpsed Monica dismount as he faded into the deeper shadows and hurried along the tree line near the water.

He waited till he was almost a quarter-mile on before he mounted. Then he put the powerful pale-bronze horse into a gallop and streaked through the rising dawn. The stabbing premonition of trouble still curled inside him, but it had no form or definition. Yet he had learned to listen to inner voices. They had served him well in the past. He leaned over and patted the powerful neck of the charging palomino. "Something's still not right, Cormac, lad," he said. "All the pieces aren't in place yet."

13

Fargo glanced at the sky. His guess had been right. It had taken almost two hours for Crawley to carefully bring up the sacks, cut them open, pour the grain out, and take the gold bars from inside. He watched as Ez strode to the trees and drove the big wagon to the edge of the lake, where he began to load the gold bars. Fargo flung a glance at Captain Billy. The man still held the Remington ready to shoot, and he was too far away to rush. He'd have more than enough time to fire a deadly dose of hot lead.

The Trailsman swore silently as Crawley loaded the last of the gold bars into the Owensboro, and he glanced at Caroline to see that her round-cheeked face held anger as well as shock now. But time was running out, he realized, and he saw Billy hand the carbine to Crawley.

"Get up," the captain said to Caroline, and reached down to help her to her feet.

"Get away from me," Caroline hissed as she shook him off and pulled herself up. She faced him, the depth of her disillusionment reflected in the bitter anger of her voice. "Who are you? Not the man I've known all my life."

"A man who saw his chance and took it," Billy said.

"No, you've turned into some kind of monster."

"You're upset. You'll feel differently when you calm down and come to your senses. Get in the wagon. We're leaving here," the captain said.

"What are you going to do with Fargo?" Caroline asked.

"Ez will see to him," Billy said.

"You can hide all kinds of things at the bottom of a lake," Crawley put in.

Caroline seemed to recoil as though she'd been physically struck, and suddenly she whirled and ran toward Fargo. "No, you can't, you can't," she shouted.

Ez Crawley raised the rifle.

"No," the captain shouted. "I'll take care of her." He darted forward with surprising speed for his short, portly shape and yanked Caroline back with one arm. "Damn you, Caroline. I planned this and went to a lot of trouble to make it work. I had to work around the damn southerners, and I'm not going to let you stand in my way. Now you're coming with me."

"No," Caroline shouted. She tried to wrest herself from his grip when a shot exploded and Fargo saw the carbine leap out of Ez Crawley's hands as his right palm spurted blood.

"Ow, Jesus," Crawley gasped out in pain, but Fargo's eyes were on the trees as the palomino came forward, the ivory-gripped Colt in Canyon's hand. O'Grady motioned to Billy with the gun and the captain let the Savage and North navy revolver fall to the ground.

"What are you doing here, O'Grady?" Billy frowned.

"It's Canyon O'Grady, U.S. government agent," the redheaded man said.

Captain Billy's eyes widened. "A government agent?" he echoed. "Jesus."

"Untie my friend Fargo and Miss Caroline," Canyon ordered, and Captain Billy undid the wrist ropes on Fargo first, then on Caroline. "Seems we made some wrong guesses, Fargo," Canyon said.

Fargo gestured to Ez Crawley. "You were right about him," he muttered.

"Which means there's still a southern agent on board," Caroline said.

"It does, and I'll go with Darlene," Canyon said. "But that's not important now. Getting that gold to a safe place is."

"I need a bandage for my hand," Crawley rumbled.

"Use your shirt," Canyon snapped.

Fargo took a step toward the wagon when he felt himself stiffen as his wild-creature hearing picked up the sound.

"Riders," he said. "Coming fast." He frowned, listened again. "From both directions," he added, and the sound seemed to suddenly explode as the riders raced through the trees.

"Damn," Canyon spit out, throwing a glance at the wagon. There was no chance to drive it away.

Fargo spun and dived headlong into the trees, rolled, and came onto his stomach where Crawley had thrown his gun belt and the knife. But he stayed in the thick foliage, the Colt in one hand now. He saw Canyon start to race the palomino along the shore, then halt and wheel the horse in the other direction as a dozen riders raced from the trees. Canyon reined up sharply and came to a stop as another dozen horsemen came up to block his path from the other side. The agent sat quietly on the horse as the young, square-jawed officer rode up to him. Canyon's eyes suddenly widened as Monica rode up between two of the troopers.

"Damn," Fargo heard Canyon curse as Monica halted, still between the two soldiers. "What'd they do to you?" he asked. "They made you talk."

"Not exactly," Monica said. "You see, it's not Monica Milford, faro dealer. It's Monica Milford, southern agent."

Fargo watched as Canyon stared at her for a long moment and then managed a wry smile as he flung a glance at Ez Crawley. "One right guess, one wrong one," he murmured.

"I'll be damned," Fargo heard Captain Billy blurt out and drew a glance from Monica. "My regular faro dealer didn't just walk out on me. You didn't just come along at the right time."

"That's right. We saw to it that he didn't come back to the boat," she said, and Fargo glanced at Caroline as she stared from one to the other and tried to take in the avalanche of twists and turns. Staying silent inside the willows, Fargo strapped on his gun belt as he watched the lieutenant move to the wagon and peer inside it.

"It's here, all of it," the young officer shouted triumphantly. "Two of you men put your tarpaulins over this wagon," he ordered, and two troopers responded at once.

Fargo returned his gaze to where Canyon and Monica still faced each other.

"I never considered you," Canyon said. "You were

very good. You even had me believing you were really saddened this morning when I told you who I was."

"I *was* saddened. I did have plans for us. You were special," Monica answered.

"Is that why you stayed after you knew, why there was one more time?"

"You know a better reason?" Monica said.

"No."

"Memories are the only things that stay. Collect them when you can," Monica said. "I'm sorry, Canyon O'Grady."

"That makes two of us," he returned as one of the troopers came up and took the ivory-gripped Colt from him.

Monica glanced at Captain Billy and Ez Crawley. "What are they doing here?" she asked.

"The good captain was behind the raids. He found out about the gold quite by accident and decided to make the most of it," Canyon said.

Monica's eyes went past Caroline, and a frown came to her brow. "Somebody's missing. Where's Fargo?" she snapped, instant sharpness in her voice.

"At the bottom of the lake," Canyon answered quickly, and threw a glance at Billy and Ez Crawley. "He came onto them fishing the sacks out, and they did him in."

Fargo's eyes went to the captain and Crawley and saw them stay silent, and he grunted in satisfaction. They had the sense to know that now he was their only chance for survival. He saw Monica's eyes go back to Canyon, probing, suspicious. "There's his horse," Canyon said, and gestured to the Ovaro. "You know he wouldn't take off without him."

Monica took another moment and finally nodded and spoke to the lieutenant. "Tie their hands, all of them," she said.

"We could use the lake for them, too," the trooper said.

"We'll find another lake. They may come in handy. Hostages do," Monica said, and shot a glance at Canyon. "Perhaps Canyon O'Grady has been in touch with more people than we know. We'll stay here till dusk. I don't want to travel by day with a wagonload of gold bars. It'd be our luck to run into a federal cavalry patrol. This operation has had one damn problem after another. Let's be careful and finish it right."

The officer nodded, ordered his men to dismount.

Fargo watched as Canyon and the others had their wrists bound. The troopers settled down beside the lake with a guard of four beside the Owensboro. Fargo strapped his calf holster on and lay down on his stomach. He stayed silent as a water moccasin in cattails.

Monica sat down not far from Canyon but studiously avoided glancing at him. Canyon lay back and rested until the day began to slide into dusk. Then he sat up and spoke to Monica.

"Are you really going to do me in, lass?" he asked almost humorously.

She shot him a quick glance. "Don't make it harder," she said.

"You didn't answer me."

"I don't have any choice."

"You sure know how to end an affair," he commented.

"Dammit, you all know too much. With you gone, we can keep on getting the gold through in the grain shipments. Somebody else will take over the boat and our lines will stay open."

"You believe in what Pierre Corneille wrote in the seventeenth century. 'Do your duty, and leave the rest to heaven,' " Canyon said.

"Shut up, damn you," Monica said as she sprang to her feet and stalked away. "Time to travel," she barked at the young officer, who rose instantly and got his troops up and mounted.

Fargo watched as Caroline was lifted onto her horse and the others pulled themselves into their saddles. One of the troopers took the reins of the wagon and two riders followed behind it.

"Move out," the lieutenant called as darkness dropped over the land.

Monica rode her horse and a trooper led the Ovaro behind him, Fargo noted as he rose and stepped from the willows. They didn't move quickly, their pace set by the cumbersome Owensboro as it wheeled through wooded terrain.

Fargo fell behind them in a steady, effortless trot. But they turned south after they came within a mile or so of the Mississippi. They were going to parallel the river all the way to St. Louis, Fargo decided. They'd continue to rest by day and move by night. Time was unimportant. Getting the gold there was what mattered.

But he had other plans, Fargo grunted grimly as he trotted after the procession. He let another hour go by, enough for the moon to rise so he could pick out the riders. He found Monica to one side, near the wagon, scanned the others, and spotted Canyon a dozen feet ahead of her, Caroline, Billy, and Ez Crawley ahead of him. Two troopers rode at each side of Canyon, he noted with a smile, and he began to edge up on the wagon. He moved to the right, went into a crouching run, and passed the Owensboro, drawing abreast of Monica, who rode with her eyes focused ahead, her lovely face set tightly. He drifted toward her through the trees. He drew the Colt as he increased speed, burst from the thick tree cover, and sprang at her, slamming into her. She flew from the saddle as the horse bolted forward.

Fargo was beside her on the ground, one arm around her neck, the Colt pressed against her temple as he dragged her back a few feet and heard the lieutenant shout a halt. He saw Canyon turn in the saddle and see him as the lieutenant rode up and skidded to a halt.

"One wrong move and she's very dead," Fargo said.

"Damn," the officer bit out.

Fargo spoke in Monica's ear, almost as though he were a lover. "Now you're going to tell them to do exactly as I say," he murmured.

She remained silent, her lips a thin line.

Fargo looked up at the lieutenant. "Everybody dismount and put down their guns," he said. "Then line up against the trees at the right."

The officer didn't move and Fargo put his lips to Monica's ear again. "I haven't been to bed with you, honey. I've no sweet memories to bother my conscience. I'll blow your lovely head off. Your people tried to kill me at least twice." He pulled the hammer back on the Colt, the sound loud as a shot in the silence.

"Do as he says," Monica said.

The lieutenant nodded, swung to the ground, and Fargo watched as he put his gun down. The other troopers did the same with their weapons.

"Against the trees," Fargo barked, and the men

lined up with proper military obedience. "Untie the others," Canyon ordered the lieutenant, and waited as the man undid Caroline's wrist ropes first, then Canyon, and finally Billy and Crawley.

"I'll be taking my gun, thank you," Canyon said, and the lieutenant had one of the troopers bring the ivory-gripped revolver. O'Grady walked to where Fargo still held the gun at Monica's temple. The agent smiled down at the young woman. "Do I perceive here 'a divided duty,' as Othello said of Desdemona?"

"What do you mean, Canyon?" Monica frowned.

"You said you had to kill me. You had no choice. It was your duty," Canyon answered. "Why didn't you tell the lieutenant to ignore Fargo's orders? It seems duty and dedication can come to a grinding halt."

"Go to hell, Canyon O'Grady," Monica hissed.

"Not yet, my lovely, not yet." Canyon laughed.

Fargo pulled Monica up with him. "Crawley, you and the captain tie their mounts together and take them away from here. About an hour away," he said.

Ez Crawley exchanged glances with Billy.

"What are you doing to do?" Billy asked.

"We'll take care of the wagon," Canyon said.

"You take their horses," Crawley growled.

Fargo moved the Colt from Monica's temple for an instant and fired, and Ez Crawley clapped a hand to the top of his ear as he yelped in pain.

"I'd just as soon shoot you as look at you, Crawley," Fargo barked. "Don't tempt me again." He saw the man swallow hard and follow Captain Billy as they gathered up the horses, tied reins together, and began to ride away, leading the two dozen or so mounts.

Fargo waited till they were out of sight and then

pushed Monica ahead of him to the wagon. "Get in," he said. She climbed into the back of the wagon and he motioned to Caroline. He handed her the big Colt as she stepped inside the wagon just behind the seat. "Keep her covered. She moves, shoot," he ordered harshly.

Canyon drew up on the palomino with the reins of the Ovaro in his hand.

"Time to go," Fargo said, and took the reins of the two horses hitched to the Owensboro. He snapped the reins hard and the animals responded.

Canyon fired a half-dozen shots toward the troopers as he rode off and watched the line of figures dive for cover. "Just to keep them in place." He laughed as he raced along beside the wagon. "Where are we going, lad?" he asked.

"To the boat," Fargo said. "Crawley and Billy won't take the horses an hour away. They'll want to come rushing back to catch up to us. I figure the Mississippi boys will have their mounts back in another hour or two and come barreling after us also."

"Meaning they'll sure catch us if we try to make it on land," Canyon said.

"Give the man a cigar. But on the boat in midriver, I figure we'll have a chance. We can pick them off easily if they try swimming out to us. We'll head straight downriver until we reach St. Louis."

"We can do better. Fort Madison's along the way," Canyon said, and Fargo nodded agreement.

He kept the heavy wagon racing through the night, crashed through brush, and found open land to go full out. He shot a glance behind every few minutes and saw Monica in the far corner across from Caroline.

She sat quietly, smart enough to know she'd no chance for anything more.

Almost two hours had gone by when Fargo saw the dark ribbon of the Mississippi and then the soft glow of light that came from the *Shady Lady* where she had been moored.

He drove the wagon to a halt at the gangplank while Canyon rode the horses on board. Four crewmen appeared, questions in their faces. "Get the passengers off. Now," Fargo shouted. "Wake them up and get them off."

"Where's Captain Billy?" one of the men asked.

"He won't be coming aboard for this trip," Fargo said, and began to unload the gold bars after stripping away the tarpaulin covers. Fargo tossed them on the deck and Canyon hauled them into the cargo area. With shouts of protest, the few passengers on board began to leave, most carrying their clothes over their arms.

Darlene appeared and Canyon paused to glance at her.

"You too, lass," he said. "And I owe you an apology."

"What are you all talking about?" Darlene asked.

"No time to explain now. Just get ashore, honey," Fargo said as he unloaded the last of the gold bars. He helped Caroline from the wagon and watched Monica climb down.

Canyon brought a length of lariat and bound her wrists together. "So you don't get foolish thoughts," he said with a fatherly tone.

Darlene, bags in hand, hurried down the gangplank.

Fargo turned to the crew. "Fire up, and keep her

fired up. We'll be moving downriver as fast as she'll go," he said. "I'll be at the wheel."

"I can take the wheel, Fargo," Caroline said. "I've done it often."

"If the time comes, honey," Fargo said, and vaulted up the steps to the pilot house. He heard the gangplank drawn in and felt the boat begin to move in minutes. He swung the wheel to port and watched the prow nose out into the river. When he reached midriver, he felt the current push at the boat and he straightened the wheel, keeping the vessel on course.

The first gray of the new day touched the distant sky as the pilot-house door opened and Canyon stepped in with Monica.

"Where's Caroline?" Fargo asked.

"Getting the ship's rifles out of the closet and putting them on the decks on both sides, loaded and ready to fire. That way we can just pick up one after the other without stopping to reload," Canyon said.

Fargo nodded to the spreading light of the dawn. "They've had plenty of time to get their horses back and come at us," he said. "I'm wondering where the hell they are."

"You'll find out," Monica said.

"You know something?" Fargo questioned.

"Just that they won't ride off and forget about it," Monica said.

"They can't wait for us to reach Fort Madison," Canyon said. "I guess that gives them another hour or so to come at us. Maybe where the river narrows or at a curve."

The new dawn spread itself across the sky and the land grew light, trees taking on shapes, hills definite contours. The great Mississippi swept onward in its uncaring, unceasing flow.

Fargo's eyes swept the shore on both sides and saw no line of horsemen race into the water. A short curve neared and he guided the paddle-wheeler around it. He felt the pull on his arms as the vessel shuddered and took the curve too fast. He had to pull hard to correct the watery skid.

One of the crewmen appeared at the door and Fargo turned to him. "The boiler's going to blow if we keep this up much longer," the man said.

"Can we get any more speed out of her?" Fargo questioned.

"A little, but not for more than another ten miles or so," the crewman said. "The paddle wheels are going so fast the paddles are going to fly off."

"Put more wood on. Give me that last bit of speed," Fargo said, and the man clattered down the steps.

The prow of the boat came around the curve, started to straighten out, and Fargo felt the curse fall from his lips. "Damn," he shouted. "There they are." The frown dug into his brow as Canyon came alongside him to stare ahead where the river narrowed.

A small town of mostly fishing boats nestled against the side of one shore, and across the river, from side to side, a line of rowboats, rafts, trees, canoes, and pieces of wood had been piled high to form a barrier. Doors had been ripped from houses, sections of fencing piled high. Fargo guessed the barrier was some ten feet high in places and perhaps six feet wide.

"They figure that'll stop us and then they can shoot their way aboard," Fargo said as Caroline entered the pilot house.

"I'd guess they've figured right," Canyon said grimly. "It'll stop us. It'll foul the paddle wheel just as one of those sawyers or sleepers would."

"Take the wheel, Caroline," Fargo said. "Just keep her in midriver." He spun, pulled Monica along as he ran from the wheelhouse. "Tie her to the rail and meet me on the main deck," Fargo said to Canyon, and raced down the steps. He found two of the crewmen and skidded to a halt. "Where are the others?" he asked.

"Feeding the boiler," one answered.

"Tell them to quit. She's going full out now. Get them up here and set fire to the boat," Fargo said.

"Set fire to the boat?" the crewman echoed, aghast at the thought.

"Like this," Fargo said, and took a wall lamp, flung it against a window, and watched it burst into flames. The fire ignited a curtain and immediately leapt along the old dry wood of the boat. He saw Canyon race up and nod with a grin, pick up another lamp, and send it crashing into flames.

The crewman raced off while the other one started for the cargo area. "There are two barrels of kerosene and a drum of oil there. Light that and you'll have the ship in flames in minutes," he said.

"Go with him," Fargo said to Canyon. "I'll get the horses over the side." He raced to the stable at the stern; both the Ovaro and the palomino were nervously pounding their hooves on the floor, already sensing danger. Fargo led both horses to the edge of the low gunwale, slapped hard against their rumps, and they dived over the rail and into the river. They'd find their way ashore and wait, he knew.

He raced back to where he'd left Canyon to see a wall of flame leap into the air and Canyon spring backward. "That's it," Fargo said. "I want this boat a huge, flaming torch when we hit that barrier. When she stops, she'll set the barrier on fire to add to things."

"And they won't have a chance in hell of getting aboard. She'll burn and sink and go to the bottom with their damned smuggled English gold. They won't get a bar of it," Canyon chortled. "The Mississippi mud will swallow up most of it and maybe the boys from Fort Madison can retrieve some tomorrow. But the South won't get it and the British lion will howl at the loss, too."

Canyon whirled as the flames spurted up from the aft section of the boat.

Fargo saw the crewmen had come to the deck and were torching the sides with oil-soaked rags wrapped around broom handles.

"Get the other side started," Fargo ordered. "Then get off the boat." He started up the steps, Canyon at his heels. "Monica's yours. Do whatever you want with her," he said, and saw Canyon halt where he'd left the young woman tied to the rail. Monica's eyes were round with fear as she saw the flames leaping up the sides of the boat.

"You can't leave me tied here, Canyon," she said.

"Ah, now, 'can't' is a harsh word, lass," Canyon said almost abstractly. "I don't think it's a word you can properly use at this time."

A tongue of flame leapt almost to the rail. "My God, Canyon, please, not this," Monica cried out. "Untie me."

"Hasty decisions are usually bad decisions," Canyon commented with a sigh, and leaned back against the side of the ship.

Fargo, racing up the last few steps, burst into the wheelhouse. The barrier was less than half a mile away now, and the sharp, acrid odor of burning wood and fabric filled the air. He glanced out the side window of the wheelhouse and saw the entire stern of the boat engulfed in flames, but the water kept the fire from the paddle wheel, which continued to churn. He took the wheel from Caroline as the boat rushed toward the barrier. "The last voyage of the *Shady Lady*," he said. "A blaze of glory it is."

Caroline's hand curled around his arm as the heat began to fill the wheelhouse and he felt the flames against the back wall. A large sheet of flame cascaded up beside the window and the small pilot house began to feel like an oven. The makeshift barrier still stretched across the river. The riverboat had become a great ball of fire, a moving fury of leaping flames with only the prow and the twin smokestacks rising above the flames and smoke.

On the shore, the square-jawed young lieutenant stared at the sight. "Son of a bitch," he muttered, but in his eyes there was a glint of admiration. "Let's ride, troopers," he said. "It's time to get back to Mississippi."

Fargo kicked the wheelhouse door open, ducked as a tongue of flame shot up, and pulled Caroline down the steps with him as fire leapt along the wood only inches from them. He reached the center deck, ran down it to find a companionway still not burned away, and pulled Caroline down with him. He reached the main deck at the prow and glimpsed Canyon on the other side with Monica. A glance upward showed the wheelhouse now a leaping mass of flame.

"Hit the water, honey," Fargo said as he jumped arm and arm with Caroline.

Monica, her wrists still bound, stared up at Canyon as the smoke and flames reached toward them where they stood at the port side of the prow, the only few feet of the boat not yet burning. "Are you going to untie me, Canyon?" she pleaded. "Or did you take me from the flames only to let me drown?"

"I'm still thinking," Canyon said. "One thing has bothered me. Where's Fullerton?"

"Dammit, this is no time for questions!" Monica shouted.

"It's a perfect time. Where's Fullerton? He was with the troopers."

"He went on to St. Louis to get things ready there," Monica shouted desperately.

"He'll have a long wait, won't he?" Canyon smiled.

"Canyon," she screamed as a streak of flame raced along the prow.

He shrugged and untied the ropes at her wrist. "I should take you in," he said. "But that would only be icing on the cake. The important part's done with."

Monica brought her hands in front of her, rubbed her wrists, and stepped onto the gunwale as another streak of flame rushed across the prow. She turned, closed her arms around Canyon's neck, and her lips were sweet and wet and warm. She pulled back, twisted, and dived into the river.

He risked another minute and watched her swim for shore before turning to race to the other side, duck leaping sheets of flame, and dive into the river.

Fargo pulled Caroline ashore with him, turned, and watched as the tremendous, sweeping ball of flame hurtled into the barrier with a thunderous crash. A hissing of flame and steam and smoke billowed up with greater force. The boat smashed more than half-way through the barrier before coming to a halt, and then there were only leaping, twisting flame and black and gray smoke.

Fargo let a deep breath escape him and saw the red-haired figure swimming toward the shore. Canyon pulled himself up beside Caroline and Fargo and turned to look back at the mass of flame in midriver.

"I didn't know you had such a flair for the dramatic, lad," he said.

"Once in a while." Fargo grinned.

"Let's get the horses," Canyon said, and Fargo pulled Caroline to her feet with him. They found the Ovaro a quarter-mile up the shoreline and the palomino only a few hundred yards away.

"I'll be riding to Fort Madison and send in my report," Canyon said. "It'll be a good one, thanks to you, Fargo, old friend."

"My pleasure," Fargo said as he gripped Canyon's outstretched hand. "We really muddled our way through, but don't tell them that."

"Never," Canyon said, climbed into the saddle, and put the palomino into a trot. He waved back before going out of sight.

"What happens to Caroline Hopkins now?" Fargo asked as she came into the saddle in front of him.

"She banked some money over the years. She'll be all right," Caroline said.

"You going to look for Captain Billy?" Fargo asked.

She thought for a moment. "No," she said finally,

the single word made of firmness. "I wonder what will happen to him."

"The Mississippi's full of old rivermen. They keep scrounging a living from it one way or another," Fargo said.

"What are you going to do now? You going on?"

"In time," he said. "But first I'm going to build another kind of fire for a while."

Caroline glanced at him, snuggled her firm, compact body against him, and drew his arm across the high, round breasts. "I promise," she murmured.

"You promise what?" He frowned.

"I won't do a thing to put it out," she said.

He smiled with anticipation as he put the horse into a gentle trot.

LOOKING FORWARD!
**The following is the opening
section from the next novel in the exciting
Trailsman series from Signet:**

**THE TRAILSMAN #101
SHOSHONI SPIRITS**

*Wyoming, 1860, the Rocky Mountain high-country,
where conniving women and dangerous men tested the
ancient Shoshoni Spirits, who passed down
terrible judgment in a cannon's roar . . .*

The Ovaro's ears perked and swiveled. Trusting his
horse's keen hearing, the big man reined to a halt and
turned to look behind him. Faint sounds spilled over
the flat top of the long rise. After a few studious
seconds, he spurred the pinto up the grassy slope until
he could see over the crest.

Less than a mile down the rutted trail, a cloud of
Nebraska dust boiled behind the unmistakable shape
of a stagecoach coming hard and fast. The bark of rifles
meant only one thing, Cheyenne, as many as twenty.

The big man rode back down to the base of the rise,
where he spurred the stallion to a gallop. Within minutes he had closed the distance and charged up the
slope to come abreast of the stage.

The man riding shotgun knelt amid luggage on the roof, firing off shots at the pony-mounted braves racing forward in the billowing dust. Passengers fired from the windows.

Skye Fargo added his Colt's firepower to that from the coach, and two half-naked Cheyenne toppled to the ground as Fargo's bullets tore into them. He reloaded while moving in closer.

An arrow streaked out of the dust. The man on the stage roof screamed and clutched his shoulder. He rolled off the luggage, but stopped short of falling off the roof.

Fargo emptied the Colt into the band of Cheyenne, holstered the weapon, and drew his Sharps from its saddle case.

Before he could fire, three Cheyenne broke from the pack and headed toward him. The war-painted riders brandished long war clubs. Fargo shot the nearest savage off his pony, then reined the Ovaro between the other two. As he charged through the tight gap, he slammed the Sharps barrel against one warrior's head, then caught the other on the chest with the backswing. Glancing over his shoulder, he watched both men roll on the sun-baked ground.

He turned the pinto to avoid the boiling dust and headed for the stage. During the movement, his keen, wild-creature hearing discerned a new sound over that made by the rumbling stagecoach and gunfire. He swerved out and glanced behind the cloud. Three horsemen chased in, firing point-blank at the unsuspecting Cheyenne. He waved for them to move right to get out of the passengers' line of fire. As a unit the three riders veered right.

Fargo reloaded the Colt while he dropped back to protect the left side of the stagecoach. With the other defenders, Fargo fired blindly into the dense, swirling cloud. Four warriors tumbled on the ground.

Contained on three sides, the Cheyenne wisely broke off their assault. They headed toward the hills and ravines to the north.

The trio of gunmen at the right rear turned to give pursuit. Fargo angled northwest to block for them. Before the Cheyenne made it to safety in gulches, three more were shot off their mounts. Fargo and the others halted.

Returning to the stage, which had stopped down the trail, the men joined Fargo. Two were rawboned youngsters, not yet twenty. Both clean-shaven young men had steel-blue eyes. Tufts of flaxen hair poked out from under the sweatbands of their wide-brimmed hats. While they weren't identical twins, Fargo guessed they might be related.

The third had a leathery face with a scar across his nose. His unruly hair, beard, and mustache were rust-colored, his sunken eyes dark-green. Fargo fixed his age at thirty-five. He doubted the man was kin to the others.

All wore brown leather gunbelts low on their hips, the bottoms of the holsters held close to their thighs with leather thongs. Each carried a single-action, five-shot Joslyn Army revolver. The youngsters, he noted, wore their guns on the left.

One of the younger men grinned as he said, "Mister, you got guts bigger'n St. Louis. I saw you takin' out them Cheyenne with that rifle. Hell, we rode on in just so we could watch you whip 'em."

Fargo chuckled. "You men couldn't have come along at a better time." He offered his hand. "My name's Skye Fargo."

"Glad to meetcha. Mine's Richard Dotson. Most call me Rick." He nodded toward the other young rider. "He's Calvin Boggs, my cousin. Cal, he don't talk much as me, but he's damn fast with a gun. Ain't that right, Cal?"

Calvin gave no indication he heard Rick brag about him. Rick looked at the older man. "That's one of our uncles, Leon McAdoo. Leon, he don't say much, either. That's 'cause some of his tongue got cut off. Where you headed, Mr. Fargo?"

"West. Yourself?"

Rick pulled on an earlobe. "Nowhere in particular. Might say we're looking around."

Fargo knew better than that. Men didn't wander just for the hell of it. They either had a destination in mind or were running, usually from the law. Whichever, it was their business. He didn't probe, although their appearance behind the stage in open country, coupled with their handiness with the Joslyns, was a mite suspicious.

At the stagecoach, Fargo was mildly surprised to see three women among the men huddled around the wounded man. They'd stretched him out on his back in a patch of shade.

One of the women, a shapely strawberry-blonde, stood next to a fleshy young brunette. A tall, willowy ash-blonde woman a few years younger than Fargo looked over the brunette's shoulder.

Fargo dismounted. The injured man's eyes were closed, his breathing shallow. An arrow was embedded deep in the flesh above and slightly left of his left breast. To pull the arrow out was unthinkable; the added damage could easily kill the man. Fargo squatted to break off the feathered fletch.

The strawberry-blonde gasped, "Sir, what are you doing?"

Fargo didn't answer right away. He lifted the man's upper torso so he could shove the arrow on through the shoulder. The unconscious man groaned. Pulling it out by the flint arrowhead, Fargo said, "Saving his life. I need a bandage." He looked up at the women. "Don't just stand there. One of you rip off a long piece of petticoat hem."

In unison they stiffened and raised their hands to their bosoms. Fargo selected the ash-blonde. "You are wearing a petticoat, aren't you?"

"Uh, er, of course," she stammered. She glanced about the faces fixed on her.

Fargo handed her his throwing knife. "Step into the stage and cut off a strip."

While she followed his orders, Fargo addressed the sweat-soaked stage driver, a short, beefy older man. "Ft. Hope's what—about an hour away?"

"More or less," the fellow grunted. "Probably more. Is Charley gonna make it?"

"He might, if you put another lather on your team. Soon as I get him bandaged to stop the bleeding, I'll ride shotgun for you."

The brunette's eyes flared. She asked, "Shotgun? Are you saying they might come back?"

"Wouldn't know," Fargo replied. "Might, might not."

The stage door opened. The ash-blonde descended, then handed a length of white material and the knife to Fargo. He tore off two pieces for compresses and used the rest to bind them in place. The two male passengers helped him lie the wounded man on the forward seat.

Fargo said, "Okay, ladies, you can get aboard now." He glanced at the two male passengers. Fargo told them to sit on the floor and hold the wounded man on the seat.

After tying the Ovaro behind the stagecoach, Fargo climbed up next to the driver. The grizzly old man snapped the reins on the horses' backs. The coach lurched forward, Dotson and his kin following.

A dusty hour later, they saw Ft. Hope, which stood on the bank of the North Fork of the Platte River. Settlers, not the military, had built the small town in the Nebraska panhandle near the Wyoming Territory. Muffled sounds of gunfire greeted the stage.

Fargo motioned for Rick to come alongside. Rick moved in and looked up at him. Fargo yelled, "How about bringing my horse to me?"

Rick nodded and fell back.

The driver asked, "What're you up to, mister?"

"I'll ride ahead to see what all the commotion's about and fetch a doc for Charley."

"Hell, mister, this is Ft. Hope. That shooting don't mean nothing. Happens all the time. Letting off steam."

"Yeah, well, I'll go check it out, anyhow."

Rick brought the Ovaro alongside. Fargo stepped down into the saddle. He dropped back to warn the women, "Be ready to duck, ladies. We're coming into town. I hear some gunfire, so I'm going ahead to make sure it's safe!" He touched the brim of his hat and galloped ahead.

Fargo entered the little frontier town on its main street. All movement had ceased. The few people he saw were crouched behind something solid, protective. The ruckus came from the crossroads near the far end of Ft. Hope. Riding toward it, Fargo saw two men sprawled facedown in the dust, and a chubby woman who sat with her back against a water trough. She was screaming and clutching her bloody left thigh. He rode by the two men, who lay in pools of muddy blood.

Closer to the crossroads, he saw, an armed man stood guard outside the door of the little bank. Seven horses were ground-reined in front of him. Without warning, the man fired at Fargo.

He dug his heels into the stallion's flanks and charged in, firing the Colt. The bullet's impact catapulted the man through the bank window.

Fargo slid from the saddle and ran to plaster his back against the outside wall of the bank. He yelled, "Throw your guns out! Follow them and you won't get hurt!"

He listened to boots scuffle on the wooden floor

inside the bank, then an exchange of whispers. A moment passed before a lone six-gun arched out through the doorway. A bearded man wearing a torn duster stepped outside.

Twin black eyes filled with meanness stared at Fargo. As the robber ducked, his hand darted inside the duster. Fargo squeezed the trigger. A nasty red hole appeared in the man's forehead. "Okay," he began, "I know there's five more of you in there. I'm giving you three seconds to come out. You can come shooting or with your hands empty. Makes no difference to me. One . . . two . . ."

By the year 2000, 2 out of 3 Americans could be illiterate.

It's true.

Today, 75 million adults...about one American in three, can't read adequately. And by the year 2000, U.S. News & World Report envisions an America with a literacy rate of only 30%.

Before that America comes to be, you can stop it...by joining the fight against illiteracy today.

Call the Coalition for Literacy at toll-free **1-800-228-8813** and volunteer.

Volunteer Against Illiteracy. The only degree you need is a degree of caring.